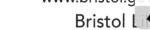

Renew by phone or online
0845 0020 777
www.bristol.gov

Bristol Libraries

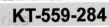

KT-559-284

PLEASE RETURN BOOK BY LAST DATE STAMPED

ISLAND OF DREAMS

ISLAND OF DREAMS

HELEN MCCABE

THORNDIKE
CHIVERS

This Large Print edition is published by Thorndike Press, Waterville, Maine, USA and by BBC Audiobooks Ltd, Bath, England.
Thorndike Press, a part of Gale, Cengage Learning.

ALL RIGHTS RESERVED
The text of this Large Print edition is unabridged.
Other aspects of the book may vary from the original edition.
Set in 16 pt. Plantin.
Printed on permanent paper.

LIBRARY OF CONGRESS CATALOGING-IN-PUBLICATION DATA

McCabe, Helen, 1942–
    Island of dreams / by Helen McCabe.
        p. cm. — (Thorndike Press large print gentle romance)
        ISBN-13: 978-1-4104-1834-0 (hardcover : alk. paper)
        ISBN-10: 1-4104-1834-0 (hardcover : alk. paper)
        1. Large type books. I. Title.
    PR6113.C35I75 2009
    823'.92—dc22   2009014336

BRITISH LIBRARY CATALOGUING-IN-PUBLICATION DATA AVAILABLE

Published in 2009 in the U.S. by arrangement with Helen McCabe.
Published in 2010 in the U.K. by arrangement with the author.

U.K. Hardcover: 978 1 408 44244 9 (Chivers Large Print)
U.K. Softcover: 978 1 408 44245 6 (Camden Large Print)

Printed in the United States of America
1 2 3 4 5 6 7 13 12 11 10 09

ISLAND OF DREAMS

1

Carla Taylor really didn't need her cardigan as she carried out the board and placed it on the pavement in front of her shop. She smiled as the light wind ruffled her hair.

Above her, the palm trees bowed their heads to the sea breeze, which swept over the broad tiled paseo, the walkway that stretched for a mile curving around the beach. The sea-front was almost deserted that morning, except for joggers who made their way steadily, one after the other, towards the yacht harbour.

However, in a month's time, Santa Eulalia would be seething with tourists, a haven for sun-seekers all over the world and Carla's shop beside the pretty block of tourist flats, which looked out on one of the best views on the island, was in a prime position. She'd been so lucky to get it!

Carla stared up at the sky. She could feel summer was on its way, although on this mid-May morning, the sun, which was climbing up from behind the mountain towards its zenith, was partly hidden by some ominous storm clouds.

Still savouring the breeze that caressed her face, she sat down on her chair, which was tucked into the little alcove beside the pavement. It was always a good idea to sit outside, as it encouraged business. People would often stop to chat and then walk inside to look round. Carla had learned a lot since she'd become a business woman.

"Hola!" She greeted Sancha from the pharmacy next door, who was doing the same thing. "Do you think it's going to rain?" Her friend shook her head.

"This isn't England! We may not be having as good weather as usual, but it won't rain." Sancha seemed very certain. "Anyway, I have to go to the dentist this morning. The other pharmacist is taking over. We'll get some business after lunch, I expect."

Neither Carla nor Sancha took a siesta. The custom was going out of fashion and mainland Spain was doing its best to persuade all shops and stall holders to stay open from one until three. It was a commercial decision. But old habits died hard and many of the shopkeepers in the street retired to rest during those peak hours of high sun — much to the tourists' disgust.

Carla looked around at her little shop. She was so proud of it. After Jack died, following much soul-searching and lots of heartache, she'd decided to come out to Ibiza, the place where they'd had so many happy holidays, and start a small business with some of the insurance money she'd received.

Now here she was on her special Mediterranean island, starting a new chapter in her life; doing what they had planned to do all along after falling in love with the place several years ago. She had never believed things would end this way, but she had to honour the promise she'd made him in hospital.

"I want you to do it, Carla, I really do. Promise me you'll go on with it!" He had held her hand so tightly and she'd looked into his earnest brown eyes, thinking that there was no way she could ever do it without him. But she'd found the strength to keep her promise.

It had been a life-changing decision, leaving friends and family behind for Ibiza. But it was what she wanted — to make a fresh start — and here she was, selling lots of different knick-knacks, candles, small gifts, pictures and, upstairs, a range of women's fashions.

Carla pushed back her dark curls, which the wind was blowing everywhere, and squinted as the sun came out suddenly and warmed her through. This had been both their ambition — to retire to this lovely island — but the dream had only come true for her.

Sometimes, she could still hardly believe that she was alone, a widow at 25, since a serious illness had deprived her of the love of her life. But it happened and, although she was still grieving, she was doing something for herself. She was determined that her new business wouldn't fail. Opening her eyes, she was delighted to see a couple standing by her chair, looking through the window. Definitely English, thought Carla.

She was right. They were Northerners. Carla couldn't tell whether Yorkshire or Lancashire.

"Are you open, dear?"

"Of course, I was just enjoying the sun," she said, looking up.

The woman bought a pretty top and two of her best candles. Carla placed the Euros in her till and smiled. Her first sale of the day and she was sure it wouldn't be the last. A moment later, a grimacing Sancha waved to her as she went past the window. Like Carla, she wasn't fond of the dentist!

Carla was just about to go and sit outside again, when a wonderful silver sports car drew up in the narrow street. Most of the vehicles in Ibiza were rattletraps, given that the drivers drove them crazily with little concern for anyone in front or behind them and usually had the dents to prove it.

It wasn't only the car that caught Carla's eye, but the occupant. The man was about her age, maybe a little older.

Dark and lithe, the suit he wore shrieked designer, as did the sunglasses. Someone used to the island would label him as a resident of the interior, or belonging to the mountain clan, where some pretty expensive villas could be found. Of course, he could have been a tourist, but he didn't look like one. Everything about him exuded wealth.

He sat for a while with the door open on to the pavement, which Carla thought was fairly annoying as no one could get past, come in her shop, or look in her window.

He had some kind of plan in his hand and, just as she was psyching herself up to ask him if he'd mind shutting his door, he jumped out, shoved the papers into his briefcase and glanced her way. He was very tall for a Spaniard. She wondered briefly how he managed to wind his legs into the confined space of the car.

Then he smiled. So she smiled back. After all, he might be a customer. In your dreams, thought Carla. Her stock was fairly good, but probably not good enough for him. But he was coming in! He was even better looking close up and when he took off his glasses, his eyes were large and dark. He was extremely dishy.

"Good afternoon." His English was very good too — hardly a trace of an accent. Carla replied cheerfully as he wandered about looking at her goods. She was a little surprised when he bounded up the stairs to Ladies' Fashions. A lot of her stock had been brought over from England on her last trip and was designed to appeal to the mature woman. To her utter surprise, he came down holding a black pashmina. It was good quality, but certainly not cashmere. In fact, she had bought the scarves in Spain from the wholesaler she used and it was marked like most items, *Made in China*. Whoever could he be buying it for?

He grinned in a friendly manner as he handed it over to be wrapped. Carla had designed her own wrapping paper and she made quite a fuss over the item as she tied it with a silvery string and presented him with it.

"Thank you." He paused. "You're English." It wasn't a question.

"Yes."

"And what brings you to our island?" The use of 'our' reminded Carla of the royal 'we'. It sounded like he owned it.

"I've been here for some time."

"Unfortunately, I haven't," he replied. "I've been on the mainland for too long."

"I see," she replied, not expecting an explanation.

"I have business interests here."

"Really? In what line?"

"Property." What else? thought Carla. "Nice shop." His smile was wonderful.

"Thank you." Moments later, he roared off, the sound of the racing engine reverberating throughout the old building. He certainly drove like a Spaniard!

At half-six and fairly weary, Carla closed up and made her way to the little restaurant on the ground floor of the block of flats where she lived. El Paso was buzzing. Like everywhere in Spain, the evening brought people out to dine in streets and cafés.

"Good day?" called Teresa, who was serving.

"Yes," replied Carla, sitting down in her usual place. Five minutes later, she was drinking a glass of good red wine and nibbling tapas. Soon, she was feeling relaxed.

At least, until Mercedes walked in.

The lawyer was looking smart in a dark tailored suit and white shirt; in fact, so smart that Carla was conscious of her faintly gipsy-dishevelled look. It suited her shop, but not smart Ibiza Town, where Mercedes had her office.

Every time that Carla visited she was conscious of how well the girl had done for herself. But she came from a rich family and knew everyone.

"May I sit here?" asked Mercedes. Her English was perfect and and had been for as long as Carla had known her. She'd engaged Mercedes when she had bought the business and had used her many times since for commercial affairs. Carla couldn't say that she was keen on the girl, but she was so efficient that it would have been madness to have found someone else.

"Of course," replied Carla. "Have you only just finished work?" Mercedes nodded and gave her order in rapid Spanish to Teresa.

"Si, it's been a heavy day. I'm glad you're here because," the lawyer leaned forward, "I have something to tell you that might be of interest." Her dark eyes gave nothing away, although something inside Carla hinted there might be trouble brewing.

14

"I had a visit today. From a friend. Not a client. I wouldn't have been able to tell you this otherwise." Carla knew then that this might be bad news. "He told me that Dona Ximene Alvarez is contemplating selling or demolishing some of her holdings."

"Oh?" said Carla quietly, but her stomach lurched. She rented her little shop from the lady in question. Indirectly, of course. She had never done business with Dona Ximene personally, who had several agents representing her.

Dona X owned an enormous amount of land in the small coastal town, like many other Ibicencan women. These ladies were immensely rich. It was a known fact that, culturally, daughters had not been prized highly when the island was just a quiet, remote place. Also the land around the coast was the poorest, quite unlike the fertile land deeper within. On account of this, the peasant farmers had bequeathed the poor land to their daughters and the rich to their sons.

However, none of these short-sighted men had foreseen the boom in tourism and, now, their daughters had reaped a fortune from selling their poor land to eager property developers and had the last laugh on their men. Such a woman was Dona Ximene,

who was the nearest to royalty the island af-
forded.

"Did you hear what I said?" asked Mercedes. Carla came to.

"Yes. I was just thinking about the shop."

"That's why I told you."

"But my lease doesn't expire for ages,"
added Carla. It was the worst news Mercedes could ever have given her.

"I didn't say she had an eye on your shop."

"Do you know that for certain?" asked
Carla anxiously.

"I don't, I'm afraid," replied Mercedes.
"But I shall keep my ears open." She sighed
and her lips twisted into a regretful smile.
"Of course, your shop is in a prime position. So near the sea and the harbour. I
can't imagine what the Dona's plans are,
but let's hope it's not that she's looking for
an extension of the waterfront. Anyway, my
advice at present is that you should wait
and see what happens."

After Mercedes left, saying she had a
dinner-date, and when the sunset was bath-
ing the houses and hotels in a rosy-red glow,
a disheartened Carla pulled on her fleece
and walked out of El Paso.

Her shop was close to the yacht harbour
at the nearest end of the half-moon beach,
which stretched for almost a mile, curving

16

around the town. Already, the lights were on in the fashionable villas that were built on the high hills above the resort.

Gosh, if I were really rich, she said to herself, looking up into the distance, I'd buy that one right at the top. Its lights were very clear. Probably security. And Carla knew why.

She and Jack had often driven up the hills in their small hired car and gasped at the luxurious mansion that lounged at the top of about two hundred white stone steps. They could see that it had an infinity pool, the edge of which cascaded down in a waterfall, while all the walls were covered in wonderful bougainvillea blooms.

She sighed, bringing herself back to stark reality. All I'm worried about, she added mentally, is losing my shop, never mind dreaming about fancy living. Whatever am I going to do if the gossip about Dona X is right? She frowned.

Minutes later, she was standing outside her shop again and looking up at her little flat above it. She felt she didn't want to go in yet, because her mind kept churning over all the possibilities.

She always tried to get some exercise before she went to bed. Maybe a stroll right now would lift her mood? But she was so tired. I won't go my usual way tonight, she decided, just amble down and have a look at the yachts.

The breeze was still blowing, but it was much less kind than the morning one. Its stiffness against her face soon began to clear her head. At least, if she had to return to England, she still had some of Jack's life insurance money left and, with the compensation she was sure to receive for the shop, she would manage.

I'll have to put up with it, if it happens, she sighed, but I don't want to leave here. The reality was that her good memories were all tied up in the island. All her dreams.

Walking slowly down the almost deserted street, she reached the railings and stood staring across the sea, her head full of those happy times. She could hear Jack's voice in her head as they'd stood there early in January, on the 6th to be exact — Epiphany — the island's Christmas.

"Look, darling, the boats are coming in."

"Do you think it's too dark for the pictures?" Carla had asked, peering across a dark Mediterranean, which was crusted by tiny, white waves.

"No," Jack had replied confidently with camera at the ready.

That night had been magical. The mayor

had built a fire on the beach to welcome the Three Kings, who brought presents for all the children. Around the glowing brazier, children were jumping about excitedly and shouting, as the fishing boats came in.

Carla felt part of it all; almost as if she wasn't a stranger. "The costumes are wonderful," she said, as the Kings came ashore dressed in clothes that had been used for centuries.

Soon, they were settled on their thrones and the noisy cavalcade was wending its way through the narrow streets with children and adults alike being showered with multi-coloured sweets thrown down by the Kings' retainers.

"Yes, it was magical, Jack," whispered Carla as she stood there, huddled against the wind. Losing him still hit her, but she was getting over it, although she talked to him sometimes. However, that cold ache in her chest for him was receding and she was warming to the joy around her. She was beginning to feel alive again.

She strolled through the marina, watching the water lapping the side of the boats, reading the names and wondering what it would be like to own one. Many of them had been moored there over the winter months at an enormous fee, while others appeared to have only just arrived.

The yachts always looked fantastic. Most seemed to be German registered, but one, in particular, caught her eye. It had a prime position and was flying the red and black Spanish flag. Its name, *La Paloma,* was painted on the side underneath a beautiful, white dove. On the extensive upper deck was positioned a small, round, pretty table, covered in a lace cloth that fluttered in the wind, but was protected from the worst by the bulkhead.

The two cushioned easy chairs were empty, but the table was laid sumptuously and there was an ice bucket on it, with a bottle of champagne poking out of the top.

Inside the yacht, she could see a white-coated waiter moving about, but no sign of the occupants. Someone's going to have a lovely dinner, thought Carla enviously, thinking of what food she had in her cupboard inside the small flat over the shop. Looks like pasta again!

Feeling thirsty, she decided to go into the small café at the end of the harbour. It was flying a flag too, but one somewhat less smart, emblazoned with a mini shark.

Elena was the haunt of deep sea fishermen, divers from the nearby diving school and yacht masters, as well as tourists in the season, many of them English, searching for the traditional fish and chips.

Carla didn't mind going in on her own, as quite a few people in town knew who she was by now. Anyway, she wasn't shy. If she had been, she'd never have dared to move to Ibiza on her own.

That night, the café was full of locals staring at a football match on the television and a light haze of smoke drifted about and mingled with the smell of frying fish and aromatic coffee. The long space was divided into two, the end partitioned off in which stood a pool table.

She pushed through the crowd at the bar, perched herself on an empty stool and smiled at the proprietor, who was a bit of a rough diamond, with a shaved head and earrings. He was a German, but he spoke English as well as Spanish.

"Good evening, Kurt."

"Hi, Carla. Good day? Are you eating?" He grinned.

"Not for a while?" she said. "Just a black coffee, please." She waited, curling her legs around the bar stool, not conscious of a man, glancing at her from the other part, divided by the bead curtain, which swung lightly in the wind.

"Thank you." She sipped the steaming hot

liquid, lost in her own thoughts, especially what Mercedes had suggested about the proposed harbour development. How would Kurt take it, she wondered. Definitely, it would make a great difference to Elena. He might even have to close down. She thought she might slip in when it was quieter and see if she could find anything out from him. Then she felt a movement at her elbow.

"Hello." The voice was deep and resonant. She started and looked round.

"Oh . . . hello!" She almost added, *What are you doing here?* He looked just as gorgeous as when he'd bought the pashmina from her that morning, but he wasn't wearing the suit anymore. Instead, he was dressed casually but, once again, his jeans shrieked designer and his T-shirt was no different. The logo was doubtless the real thing. A soft, navy, cashmere sweater was slung over his shoulders and knotted by the arms in front.

"May I join you?"

"Yes, fine." He pulled over a vacant stool and sat down opposite, winding his long legs around it.

At that moment, she was extremely conscious of how she looked.

"Would you like anything else?" he asked, looking down at her coffee, then up into her eyes. His own were dark and luminous. Spanish men were so up front!

"No, thanks, I'm off home soon," she replied lightly to cover her confusion. He was still looking straight at her.

"And where's home?" He seemed sincerely interested, but she needed to be cagey. He could have been anyone. But, inside, she knew he was the real thing. An aristocratic Spaniard.

"Just over there," she said vaguely, glancing out of the door, determined to give nothing away. She was sorry a moment later, when he confided, "I'm out there too. On a yacht." She bristled a little at his arrogance. I might have guessed he'd have one of those, she thought. It would match the car. Yet, the whimsical smile on his face showed he was trying to be friendly. She thawed.

"I've just been looking at them. Do you live on yours permanently?" She didn't mean to sound scathing, but he didn't seem to notice.

"No, remember I told you I'm from the mainland. But I have family connections to the island." Then he changed the subject. "Was business good today?"

"Not too bad actually. I think I'll survive." She could hear the edge come back into her voice.

"I'm glad to hear it," he replied, unwinding his long legs from around the stool. "Anyway, what are you doing this evening?"

Her heart gave a funny little jump. Was he about to ask her out?

"Not much. Just going home to eat." She put down her cup and she saw him glance at her wedding ring, which she would never take off. Of course, he thought she was married! He was wearing a gold band too. Then she remembered that Spaniards wore their wedding rings on the right hand.

"So am I. Not that I have anything against Kurt's food." He leaned over conspiratorially. "But I'm not a chip man."

You don't look it, she thought, but added, "I like his omelettes." He laughed.

"Spanish ones, I hope!" He had a marvellous smile, which lit up his face.

"Something like that." She was suddenly at a loss. She stood up, and he vacated his stool as well. They stood looking at each other for a brief moment, then Carla felt she had to break this awkward moment.

"I have to go now."

"You know something?" he said quickly. She knew instinctively that it was a delaying tactic.

"What?" she smiled.

"We haven't been introduced properly." He gave a tiny bow, and his eyes were dancing mischievously. He began, "I'm Felipe . . . Xavier . . . Darien . . . Juan . . ."

"Please stop," she said, laughing. "How many names do you have?"

"I'm sorry. I have eight in all. Shall I go on?"

She couldn't help laughing

"I'm afraid I only have two." She put out her hand and he took it. "Carla Jane Taylor! How do you do, Felipe . . . Xavier . . . ?" she frowned mockingly.

"Stop," he said. "I asked for that, didn't I?"

"I'm afraid you did." He was still holding her hand in a firm, warm grasp. She looked down and he let go. She felt her face going red. This is ridiculous, thought Carla, I'm behaving like a teenager. Her heart was pounding.

Totally conscious of him walking behind her, Carla stopped outside the door. "Well, it was nice meeting you," she said awkwardly.

"Would you care for a stroll on the paseo?" He glanced at his watch and she knew, instinctively, that he had time to spare.

And I'm not going to fill it, she thought, defensively.

"Not tonight," she replied. "I've some-where to be."

"Ah, I understand. It's a pity. I would have liked to talk to you some more." He offered his hand again. She reciprocated. "I hope we meet again, Carla."

"I'm sure we shall," she replied, knowing that she sounded frosty.

"Manyana?" He had that little boy look again.

"Perhaps."

"Good. Then I must leave you. But I was very happy to see you again." And, to her utter amazement, he drew her to him and kissed her on both cheeks. She felt her cheeks flaming. It was no big deal. The Spanish always greeted and said goodbye to each other like that.

He let her go and she found herself breath-less. With a tiny wave of his hand, he turned and walked off without looking back.

Carla stood there for a moment, feeling cross with him and herself. He'd evidently only asked her to go for a walk with him, because he was filling in time. When she got her breath back, she told herself off for being so silly. What did any of it matter? What on earth was the matter with her? She'd only met the guy twice and here she was, reading all kinds of things into his behaviour.

Then, seconds later, she began to feel guilty. It was almost as if she was letting Jack down. She felt so confused. She breathed in deeply and let out a little sigh. Maybe it would always be like this? Carla walked back in the direction of the shop. Suddenly, she saw a familiar figure walking towards her.

Mercedes was click-clacking along in the highest heels Carla had ever seen. She looked stunning in a short black dress, holding a tiny bag and wearing a beautiful jacket to complement the ensemble. Her long black hair cascaded over her shoulders and, as they came face-to-face, Carla saw her make-up was impeccable.

"Hi," she said, "you look great. Going somewhere nice?" She was hoping to find out just where the lawyer was headed, but she was disappointed as the girl only smiled and said,

"Yes. Thank you. Can't stop. Bye!"

"Bye," called Carla, watching her neat rear enviously as Mercedes hurried past. Gosh, she wished she looked like that after work!

Half an hour later, Carla was back in her flat, curled up on the settee, with a glass of red wine beside her, eating spaghetti Bolognese and watching television. But she couldn't concentrate on the programme, as her mind kept flicking back to the day's events.

At least, Mercedes's worrying news had been somewhat eclipsed by the two meetings with the handsome 'Felipe of the eight names'! She wondered who was in line for the pashmina. His girlfriend — he must surely have one — or even two! She couldn't imagine that. His mother then?

She smiled as she washed up. Suddenly, she felt most terribly alone. Then she shook off the feeling. Tomorrow was another day and, if it was as interesting as today had been, then she mustn't be too upset.

2

It was going to be a lovely day. Carla stood on her tiny terrace in her pyjamas and breathed in the fresh sea air. As a rule, she loved the way the morning sun bathed the old buildings opposite her in the most wonderful light. On this lovely island, it was a bonus to be enjoyed, unless one hadn't slept well. And she hadn't. She yawned and stepped back inside.

Half an hour later, she was still yawning as she came down her stairs and unlocked the shop door to be met by the highly pungent smell of the candles. Carla felt suddenly dizzy. She'd also washed last night's dinner down with three glasses of red wine. She drank very little usually and, when she had more than one glass, it didn't suit her.

"Phew" she sighed, going over to the shop window. The yellow peasant sun dress strung out across its length, its skirt strewn with the tiniest of yellow and blue shells, suddenly seemed a bit dated. She'd promised herself that she would re-dress it during the week but, at that moment, she didn't feel particularly creative.

But she soon came out of her dozy state, when she saw what was happening outside. On the other side of the street, three men were standing and, beside them on the pavement, was a heap of free-standing equipment and silver cases.

"Oh, no," said Carla out loud, "they look like surveyors." She was fully awake now. She watched one bend down and start setting up. "It must be true," she said, "they're surveying the marina."

At that moment, she wanted to march right outside and demand to know what they were doing but, luckily, commonsense prevented her. They were Spanish and hers didn't stretch to technical matters and, besides, they probably wouldn't tell her anything.

If this had been England, she'd have been able to go down to the Planning Office and find out, but, here, she just didn't know what to do. A trip to the local Town Hall in the square seemed easy, but the red tape inside was insurmountable, unless you knew what you were doing.

She opened the door and looked to see if

Sancha had opened yet. No! Mercedes was her only hope. Carla looked at her watch. The lawyer usually began her day's business fairly early.

Carla's phone call was rewarded by an answer phone, which announced that Mercedes would not be in the office all day, but a message could be left for her and would be forwarded to her mobile.

Carla complied. Afterwards, she wondered if she'd sounded panicky and, maybe, rather foolish. Then she remembered Kurt. Maybe she would go and find him, but he didn't open until the lunchtime rush. There was nothing for it. She'd have to sit it out.

She spent an agonised couple of hours, not made up for by many customers, watching the men, measuring and peering through their theodolites. She'd enlisted Sancha's help finally, who'd had a word with them and had got absolutely nowhere. Her friend had shrugged her shoulders and said she'd have to speak to her husband. She evidently wasn't that concerned. After all, she only worked for the pharmacy, not owned it. At eleven, Carla had had enough. She finally decided to close and go shopping. After all, she'd eaten everything edible in the flat last night.

Come on, girl, she said, as she walked up

to the main street, you've been in a worse situation than this before. British, you may be, but you're not going to take this sitting down!

She came out from a side street into the main thoroughfare of the little town. Every road led from the sea into the square. It was all very simple. No one could get lost.

The broad avenue was lined with all kinds of shops, big and small. The most delicious smells wafted in the air as she passed her usual baker's, making a mental note not to forget her bread on the way back — and not to bring home one of the cakes she liked the most, which were shockingly fattening.

She lingered outside one or two souvenir shops, sizing up the opposition and, the sight of one of the multi-coloured pashminas on offer, found herself remembering him.

Carla wondered if his date had gone well. It was probably a date. How would somebody like the handsome Spaniard not have a wife or a girl friend? She walked on towards the small supermarket and hovered outside. Water? She'd need to leave that until last — it was so heavy. In fact, why didn't she pop in for a coffee first, then get her shopping?

The town had many restaurants and coffee shops. When she and Jack had arrived first, they must have tried them all out and whittled their favourites down to two! Which one today? First class or ordinary?

If she went for first, she might miss a morsel of local gossip as to what was going on in the harbour. On the other hand, the best was quite often the most useful. Lots of ex-pats frequented the place, rich villa owners, who had the ear of officials. It was Mercedes' favourite haunt as well. Maybe, just maybe, the lawyer might be hanging out there on her day off.

The coffee bar and restaurant enjoyed a great situation on the corner of the main crossroads in the town. The one end of the cross went down to the sea along a palm-tree lined avenue; the other led up to the wooded mountain on which a pretty white church was placed.

Carla had walked up there with Jack several times, before he became ill. She pushed the thought out of her mind as she walked in under the striped awnings fluttering in the breeze, and sat down at a small table for two and looked around.

The seats were filling quite rapidly. Several well-dressed Germans, who looked like businessmen, were in a huddle at one of the corner tables. Next to her was sitting an elderly woman with a small, pampered dog, which wore a jewelled collar, but there was no sign of Mercedes.

Carla was looking at her watch as the white-shirted waiter came out, balancing a tray expertly. Juan smiled at her as he passed, his eyes flicking her the message he would serve her next.

A moment later, he was back. "Capuccino, please, Juan." They exchanged the usual pleasantries and, sighing, Carla sat back in the shade of the awning, watching the increasing traffic and waiting for her order.

Her heart almost stopped as the roar of an engine brought several heads swivelling around. She couldn't believe it. Him again.

She drew back involuntarily as the driver brought the car perfectly into the tiniest of parking places, jumped out and walked across the square, carrying a briefcase. A moment later, he was sprinting up the steps of the Town Hall, which was the focal point of the town. Its red, black and yellow flags were flying briskly in the breeze and, as always, it was guarded by two policemen, who made sure no one parked too near the imposing steps.

Good, he hasn't seen me, thought Carla but, inside, a tiny voice was telling her that she wished he had. She wished that he would come over and sit down opposite her! You're being so silly! Why should he see you? Why would he even want to? She was still telling herself off sternly, as the coffee arrived.

Sipping it, she kept glancing across towards the beautiful open sports, which was attracting a lot of attention even on this wealthy island. Boys walked around it lovingly; old men lingered, then walked on enviously and even the Germans pointed it out and nodded approvingly.

He's been in there a long time, she thought. He's probably at a meeting. As she was trying to decide whether to re-order, he reappeared. She had been making the other cup last out and trying to remember all his names. His first was easy, Felipe, Philip in English, but the rest . . .

The Spaniard stood talking and joking on the steps with one of the police guards, looking absolutely wonderful. He was wearing casuals again. Perfect trousers, lovely pale blue shirt, fashionable linen sports jacket, designer glasses and smart sandals. Nodding amiably to the policeman, he came down the steps and walked over to the car.

Disappointment welled up. No, he hadn't noticed her. But he was only putting his briefcase inside the boot! Seconds later,

Carla was holding her breath and trying to look nonchalant, as he approached.

"Hola," he said, with a tiny bow. "May I?" He indicated the empty chair.

"Of course," replied Carla, catching a glimpse of the rich, old lady's expression at the neighbouring table. Even she was smitten.

"I think we are fated to meet, Carla," he added, smiling. He'd evidently remembered her name! "Would you like another coffee?"

"Please, Felipe."

Felipe flicked a gesture towards the restaurant door and Juan appeared, like a genie, in response, waiting for the order. "Two coffees." He drank his black.

Everything about the man was fascinating. His lithe brown hands as he used them expressively to talk, his piercing brown eyes, bordering on coal-black. His strong, high cheekbones and his fluid mouth. At one point, Carla found herself thinking about kissing him.

He was also an excellent listener and, soon, the matter that had been plaguing her mind since her conversation with Mercedes the day before, came tumbling out — although Carla was switched on enough to realise that maybe with his connections he might know something about the redevelopment.

"I have a lot of sympathy with you, Carla," he said, leaning back easily in the chair, his eyes caressing her face. "My business interests are international and I don't know how many times, I have faced planning issues. But I did something about it. I pushed and pushed, until I got what I wanted."

"I'm sure you did," responded Carla, wanting to add, the difference is, you have a lot of money and, I expect, power. People listen to you. I'm only a small shopkeeper in a foreign country. But she didn't say it.

Instead, she asked, "What do you do exactly? I think you told me some kind of development."

He smiled. "Unfortunately, I am a lawyer, specialising in estates and property."

"Why unfortunately?"

"Lawyers are not popular people," he grimaced.

"Is that so? I think they're useful," she smiled — and would have dearly liked to have added, And very rich! "I wonder if you know my solicitor?" she added. He lifted his eyebrows questioningly.

"Mercedes Carrea?"

"I've met her."

"Then she works in your area?"

"Yes, she does, I believe." Carla could see by his face that he didn't intend to enlarge on the subject.

"She says she doesn't know if anything is going on with the project that was mentioned concerning the marina . . ." He made no comment. "I don't really know how to proceed."

"I think you need to wait a little while. In the end, someone is sure to tell you what is going on."

"But this is my livelihood. I'm worried. I've sunk all my cash into the venture." She didn't want to sound desperate, but she was sure he thought she was.

"It's a very nice little business," he said, "and in a prime position. In my opinion, you should sit it out until you hear otherwise. Spanish planning is a very long process."

"That's what Mercedes said," she sighed. "I know I shouldn't ask you," Carla began, "but I did see you going into the Town Hall. Do you know anything about the marina development?"

His expression had become serious. "If I did, I couldn't tell you. Client confidentiality and all that."

"I'm sorry. I shouldn't have asked." Carla was disgusted with herself.

"But . . ." he seemed to be considering what he should say next. "But, if it makes you feel any better, I am not in favour of changing the face of this island. I grew up here and I like it just as it is." She knew she was staring at him. "Have I said something wrong?"

"No, it's just . . . just that you speak such good English," she said to cover how she was feeling. Somehow, his declaration had made her feel much better.

"Thank you. I read International Law at Madrid and one of my years was spent in England at Oxford."

"I'm afraid my Spanish is rather basic," she replied, "which makes some things rather difficult."

"I can imagine," he replied and, a moment later, to Carla's utter surprise, his hand slid over hers and squeezed it in a sympathetic gesture. She couldn't believe how much that slight touch affected her, even when it was withdrawn. It left her trembling inside, hoping that her face would not betray her feelings.

As Carla tried to recover, he added, "I hope you don't think this is a brutal question . . ." She wondered what was coming, ". . . but why are you here alone, with all this worry?" He must have caught her look, because he continued hurriedly. "I should not have asked."

"No, it's perfectly all right," she said. "I came out here after my husband died." As she said it, tears flooded her eyes. It was so ridiculous, not to be able to hide her feelings. Even now!

"I'm sorry," he apologised. "It was unforgivable of me to upset you." His brown eyes caressed her gently.

"No, I'm being stupid. It's been a long time. Jack had leukaemia. You know . . ." She trailed off.

"Yes, I know." They sat in silence, with Carla cursing herself for being so emotional. She still couldn't talk about Jack's death to anyone without getting upset. When was she going to get over it? "I don't think anyone does," he said suddenly.

"Pardon?"

Was he reading her thoughts?

"Get over someone's death, especially one so dear." She nodded. "I lost my father when I was young. I think of him many times." His unconscious slip of English was endearing. He was being so nice. Somehow, she felt they had drawn much closer, almost as if they had known each other for ages.

Suddenly, he looked at his watch. "Oh," he said, "forgive me, Carla. There is somewhere I have to be!" Before Carla could reply, he clicked his fingers and Juan re-appeared.

"No, please I can pay for myself . . ." she began. Felipe raised his eyebrows.

"No, no," he murmured, throwing several notes on to the tray. Then, suddenly, he was staring straight into her eyes. "Next time, I hope we shall not meet by chance. If you are free, perhaps you would do me the honour of dining with me tonight? I could pick you up at — say — eight? Then I shall not be in a hurry and, hopefully, I will be able to make your troubles lighter."

She felt her stomach flip. "That would be lovely," she replied weakly.

"Perhaps you may tell me where you live?" His eyes twinkled.

"In the flat over my shop," she replied.

"Thank you." He bent over and actually kissed her hand! It was so sweet. "Adios. Until tonight."

"Until tonight," echoed Carla. "I shall look forward to it." As he smiled and put on his dark glasses, Carla caught the eye of the old lady with the dog. Her expression clearly said, *Go for it, girl. I wish it was me!*

A minute later, Carla, with most of the other customers, watched him bend and climb into the low car, rev it up and blast off across the square.

"Phew," said Carla, sitting back to collect herself for a moment . . . Soon, she was walking along the thoroughfare towards the supermarket and a quarter of an hour later, staggering out carrying her shopping, including four large bottles of water.

But her heart was lighter than her purchases. In fact, lighter than it had been ever since she had heard about the proposed marina development because, suddenly, she felt she had found someone on her side.

Someone to advise her perhaps, not legally — she couldn't imagine jettisoning Mercedes — but, at least to offer the opportunity of a fresh outlook, not only on her business problems, but also her personal life. What a change one morning could bring!

She suddenly remembered the baker's and emerged carrying two bags, one which contained her favourite cake. She was happy.

"Thank you, Felipe," Carla murmured under her breath, almost swinging the heavy water bottle carrier, "I misjudged you. You aren't arrogant at all. In fact, you seem a very nice guy."

3

Carla realised this would be the first time that Felipe had seen her looking smart. Before when they'd met, she'd been wearing her work clothes so, that evening, she took especial care getting ready.

It was such a strange feeling, going on a date, with someone you hardly knew. All her past outings had been with Jack. She panicked a little, wondering if she ought to call it off. Maybe she wouldn't know what to say?

Calm down, she told herself, as she concentrated on trying to smooth her curls. All you're going on is a date. If the two of you don't get on, so what? She also knew this wasn't true, because she really wanted him to like her.

In fact, when she thought about Felipe, her stomach gave tiny leaps. Maybe he felt the same? She laughed out loud then, No way. But he must be single, or he wouldn't have invited her out. Hopefully. Then she began to worry. Did he see her as a potential conquest? Maybe she wouldn't go, after all.

Then excitement quelled the uncertainty. At seven-fifteen, Carla was ready. She was usually punctual, but not early. Tonight was different. She kept looking down into the street to see if he had come, then going back and checking herself in the mirror.

She hadn't worn the skirt before and had bought it in a mad moment. It was one hundred per cent silk, and chocolate brown. To complement the rich colour, she had chosen a silk top in beige and a pretty, wooden necklace and bracelet to match. Probably his other girlfriends wore diamonds. On her feet were fashionable laced espadrilles.

Her hair had behaved itself at last and she was almost satisfied. Her skin was the kind that tanned and it had already acquired a glow, which she'd enhanced with bronzer. She felt she looked nice, but she was still nervous. So she made herself a cup of tea to allay the anxiety.

All at once, her nerves were compounded by the roar of an engine. "He's here," she said out loud, her panic returning. "Where's my bag?" She dashed into the bedroom, where it was sitting on the dressing table, pretty, small and bronze with a golden clasp.

Then she peeped out of the window to be rewarded with the sight of Felipe winding himself out of the sports. He was wearing a light sand-coloured suit, which looked absolutely perfect.

Breathing in deeply, Carla took one last look round her tiny flat, slipped out of the door and closed it firmly behind her.

"You look lovely," Felipe said admiringly. She thought again how unbelievably good-looking he was.

"Thank you," she smiled but, inside, she was so strung up with excitement that she wondered how she was going to get through the evening.

He was holding open the car door. She got in as gracefully as she could, which was somewhat of an ordeal, as it was so low. Then he went round the driver's side and, when he was sitting at the wheel, he turned to her. "Are you comfortable?" He grinned.

"Fine." She was now. She'd never ridden in a Porsche 911 before but, once inside, it was thrilling.

"Great." His hand lingered lovingly on the gear stick.

"Where are we going?"

"One of my favourite restaurants. It's some way from here."

"Not in town then?"

"No. The interior. It's a bit of a ride." Next moment, the engine sprung into life. It certainly was the most exhilarating ride Carla had ever taken. Breathtaking in every way — the driving, the scenery and the escort.

The island was blooming with spring blossom as the Porsche snaked its way through the hills, where tiny white-washed villages clung to the sides of the valleys.

He was a fast driver but, as Carla watched the way he handled the wheel expertly, her fear receded. He must have caught her looking.

"Don't worry. I was brought up on these roads."

"I'm not. I'm just enjoying the scenery."

"So am I," he replied, his eyes strafing her. There was no mistaking the inference . . .

The restaurant stood at the end of a deserted country lane and looked like a farmhouse, but there were some very expensive cars parked outside. The trees were festooned in fairy lights and Carla could hear laughter as she swung her legs out and stood up to find herself almost in his arms.

Carla had underestimated the surroundings and the way in which they were greeted. She felt like royalty as she was presented with a flower by the immaculately turned-out maitre'd, who turned out to be called Pedro and was the restaurateur.

They were led to a table, which was placed on a terrace with a marble floor. Carla gasped. The other side of the building overlooked a panoramic view! "I didn't know we were so high up."

"Understandable. It's very low in my car." His eyes gently mocked. The sun was setting now and, below, the valley was a dark-orange void between the mountains, punctuated by small patches of glimmering light that were villages, and larger ones that must have been towns.

After the hovering wine waiter had been given his orders, Felipe pointed, "There's Santa Eulalia."

"It's so far," she said incredulously. Carla couldn't tell where the land ended and the sky and sea began. A light wind ruffled her hair and she breathed in imperceptibly.

"Thank you," she said. His eyebrows lifted.

"What for?"

"For bringing me to such a beautiful place."

"You haven't tried the food yet," he joked.

Carla found talking to Felipe so easy that it seemed she'd known him for years. As the wonderful meal continued, the whole date began to take on the appearance of a dream.

The setting was remarkable, retaining an old world Spanish charm, simple but stunning. The food was indescribably succulent as well as a work of art and, besides, Carla knew she had an escort most women would die for.

In fact, when they'd walked in, Felipe had nodded to several couples.

"You know lots of people," she said.

"Bound to in my business," was the response. She would have been happy with a fuller answer.

"Clients?"

"Some." He evidently didn't mix business with pleasure, but she particularly noticed the effect Felipe had on some of the ladies present. Once or twice, she wondered how many girls he'd brought to the same place, but then squashed the unwelcome thought.

One woman was smiling at them right now. She was middle-aged and definitely aristocratic Spanish, and she and her companion were about to leave. Carla realised that she was coming over to speak to them.

"Dona Ana?" He inclined his head as he stood. "May I present my friend, Carla?" They exchanged pleasantries and Carla had the immediate impression she was under close scrutiny.

"How is your dear mother?" asked the lady. Carla couldn't wait to hear. She was really interested in any snip of information about Felipe and his family.

"She's very well, thank you," he replied courteously.

"Wonderful. And very busy expect." The lady smiled. "But now you are back here to help, I'm sure she'll take a break. I haven't seen her for ages. We always used to lunch, as you know." Her companion nodded in agreement.

"And I'm sure you will again," he replied sweetly. "I'll have a word with her."

Although Felipe's manner and tone were perfectly correct and polite, Carla suspected he didn't want to be discussing his mother in front of her — or anyone, in fact.

He got up and kissed both ladies on each cheek. Dona Ana smiled and looked down at her. "So charming," she murmured. "Do have a lovely evening."

"Thank you," replied Carla. With a slight wave, Dona Ana and her elegant companion moved off.

"They are very old friends of my mother and . . . exceptionally . . ." he shrugged, evidently looking for the right word. Carla would have liked to say 'nosy', but resisted.

". . . Exceptionally . . . Let's say nothing escapes their notice."

"I could see that," said Carla. "I wonder what they thought of me."

"Probably that you were very beautiful."

Carla flushed.

"But I'm afraid your presence with me will be noted and reported. I apologise in anticipation."

Carla smiled involuntarily.

"I have said something wrong?"

"No, no, it's just that I'm not used to hearing English spoken so correctly. The anticipation thing. It's good." He smiled now. She'd evidently said the right thing complimenting him on his English. "Anyway, it seems your mother has many interests." She was dying to hear more.

"Many," was the disappointing reply, as he called over the waiter. She felt slightly miffed, after the earlier warmth he'd shown, encouraging her to discuss her private problems.

He must have sensed her air of discomfort because he leaned over and said, "More wine?"

"No, thank you." He waved the waiter away.

"Please let's forget the interruptions and concentrate on us?" When he pleaded, Carla could imagine what he'd looked like when he was a little boy. Her heart softened.

"I'd like that," she replied He put out his hand and covered hers. She felt her heart flutter. Enjoy it, while you can, Carla, she thought. She closed her eyes involuntarily. His touch was what she needed.

"What are you thinking?" he asked quietly.

"That it's been a wonderful evening," she murmured in response. "Thank you again for bringing me here."

"It's not over yet," he said. "Shall I order some more coffee?"

Later, as they sipped the aromatic brew from tiny china cups, Carla found herself opening her heart to him again. At one point, she found herself thinking, I really like him, better than I've liked anyone since I lost Jack.

Felipe was so easy to get along with. So attentive and romantic. At one point, she had even said to herself, I could fall in love with him, if I wasn't still in love with Jack.

The evening passed like a lovely dream and, far too soon, Carla finally found herself sitting in his car outside her flat. The engine was still purring and a tiny touch of panic made Carla's stomach tighten. Should she ask him in? Would it be right? It certainly felt like it at that moment, but maybe she would regret it afterwards.

"Something on your mind?" he asked, his dark eyes serious.

"Nothing really, except . . ." She looked up at the flat. "Except I've had a marvellous time and . . . I . . . want to thank you . . ." Her voice trailed off, seemingly stuck in her throat.

"Don't worry. I understand," he replied quietly. "Anyway, I have an early start. Thank you too."

"What for?"

"For being such an amazing dinner date. It's a long time since I enjoyed myself so much."

She gazed at him in surprise, then realised he was leaning towards her. Her heart beat quickly as he drew nearer, then her eyes closed briefly as he kissed her lightly on the lips. Then he withdrew. "I hope we can go out again soon."

"I hope so too," she said sincerely. His kiss awoke so many forgotten feelings, bringing tiny shocks throughout her body.

As she watched him drive off, his hand flicking her a wave, she didn't know whether to laugh or cry. As she climbed the stairs, she felt more alive than she had done for a long time. And it was all because of Felipe.

4

Felipe rang her before eight, when the morning sun was turning every building and window into liquid gold. Carla listened, imagining where he was sitting, what he was doing as he phoned.

"Would you like to go out today?"

"When? I can't in the morning. I'm in the shop."

"And I'm at work," he said.

"Now?" It was very early. "In your office?" She was hoping he'd tell her where it was. Probably Ibiza Town.

"No, on my yacht. These days I'm not tied to a desk. I know. Would you like to come over and have some lunch when you close? You do take a siesta?"

"Only sometimes."

"Working too hard is bad for you."

"I'd love to come to lunch," she said. "How do I find you?"

"In the marina. I fly the Spanish flag," he

said. "I am moored in a row of Germans. A good position. First row. You can't miss me."

Carla's heart skipped. Could it possibly be the fantastic yacht she had seen before she met him? The one with the little table on the upper deck. It had been flying the Spanish flag. "Has your yacht a name?"

"*La Paloma.*"

Carla smiled. She was right! "I'll find her. What time?"

"Twelve-thirty?"

When Carla put down the phone, she was breathless. Lunch on his fabulous yacht.

It was hot and she was glad to close the shop. Custom had been slow again, but although she'd sold one or two things, her mind wasn't on her work. She couldn't settle to anything. What should she wear for her lunch date? Then she began imagining she might be one of a long string of women he entertained on his yacht.

For instance, he must have been expecting someone the night she'd gone for a walk and noticed the table and the waiter. Why did the idea upset her? You're becoming extremely silly, Carla, she told herself severely as she took one outfit down and then another.

Whatever she chose, it couldn't match his

designer labels, so she went for what she thought suited her the best. Simplicity. A silk two-piece she'd brought with her from London; aqua, with a flowing skirt that had tiny inserts to make it even more floaty.

Then she wondered if it was too dressy. By then, she was in a panic. She made herself a cup of tea and tried again. This time she chose a flowing cotton printed skirt, a camisole and a pretty shirt. That was better. Taking care over her make-up and choosing exactly the right kind of small clutch bag, she slipped out of the door.

She moistened her lips as she walked along between the yachts. Her throat felt extremely dry and her heart was pounding. He must have been looking for her because he jumped off the yacht, and came to meet her.

Soon she was seated on the top deck, under an awning, sipping a delectable cocktail. There was no sign of a waiter. They were completely alone. Carla's stomach kept doing surprising little turns.

"Are you all right?" asked Felipe. He was stirring his drink and looked every inch of a James Bond figure. Tall, dark and lean. Sophisticated too.

"Fine. It's a wonderful boat."

"I love her," he said simply. "But she can be fickle."

"How?" asked Carla, laughing at his quizzical expression.

"She does not like me cooking in her galley. Therefore, I have to send out for food. Which I have done."

"You're so funny," said Carla.

"And you are so beautiful." He must have seen her look. "I mean it. No one quite as lovely has graced this deck."

"Oh, Felipe, I think that's going too far," reproved Carla, although she was brimming over inside with happiness at the compliment.

"No, it's true. This is a new yacht. I only bought her a month ago. I have had no time to entertain beautiful women." She laughed at his teasing and they leaned back companionably.

Wherever the food came from, it was delicious. A wonderful paella and perfectly accompanying wine. A dreamlike hour passed, very different from any that Carla had experienced on the island. Afterwards, they stood very close to each other, looking out to sea.

"Are you tired?" he asked quietly, slipping his arm around her shoulder. "I have a big hammock," he joked. She couldn't see his eyes behind his sunglasses, but his lips had curved into a charming smile.

"No, I'm fine." Her legs felt weak. It was probably the wine and the excitement. He looked down at her, then took off his sunglasses. His dark eyes met hers and lingeringly held her gaze.

"I would like to kiss you again, if you will let me."

"I might," said Carla. A moment later, he took her in his arms. His kiss demanded she should kiss him back. It was a marvellous moment that was getting slightly dangerous. He must have sensed her withdrawal and loosened his embrace.

"Thank you," he murmured.

"I should go," she said.

"And leave me to my siesta?" She nodded. Then he added directly, "I would rather you spent it with me."

"I know," replied Carla, "but I'm not ready, Felipe. I'm very flattered. It's not that I don't want to . . . it's just . . . too soon . . . after Jack." There, she'd said what was really in her heart; the reason why she was holding him at arm's length. If she drove him away, then it was her fault. But she couldn't help it.

"I understand," he said, putting his glasses back on, "and I should not have asked. It's because I like you a lot. Shall I see you again?"

"If you want to." She held her breath.

"Of course I do. Come, let me help you," he said. He leaped down the stairs to the lower deck and held out his hands. She slid into his waiting arms and stood there. "I shall ring you very soon. You're good for me, Carla." He put out his hand and stroked back her hair.

"Am I?"

"Yes. Instead of taking the siesta, I shall get back to work." He grinned and indicated what appeared to be an office area, full of sophisticated communications. "I'll walk you back." He was about to leap on to the pontoon.

"No, no, I'd rather go on my own, thank you." He put his head on one side as he considered her words. Then he jumped over and held out a hand to help her. They stood hand in hand.

"Maybe you are ashamed to be seen with me?" She couldn't see his eyes.

"Of course not."

"That's all right. I'm not offended. Next time, I shall come and see you in the dark." He pulled her to him and held her tight, his lips seeking hers with an urgency she had not felt before. She responded.

He lifted her hand to his lips and she trembled inside at his hot touch. "Goodbye, Felipe and thank you again."

"Adios, Carla."

As she walked away from the yacht, she could feel him watching her, but when she turned, she just caught a glimpse of him leaping back on to the deck. She felt as though her whole body was on fire as she walked on — and not from the sun.

You've only yourself to blame if you never see him again, she told herself sternly as she turned the corner.

Actually, she saw him very soon, but not in the way she was expecting. Four in the afternoon and the surveyors were back and accompanied by a clutch of dark-suited burly businessmen, who spent a lot of time pointing and gesticulating.

Once again, Carla wished she could just go out and ask them what was going on, but it was impossible. One of them unrolled a large plan and several of the surveyors and the other men were studying it. She felt cold in spite of the sun on her back. Almost as if she had been struck by a premonition that something awful was about to happen. The whole thing looked very serious indeed.

Sancha came out of the pharmacy and

walked up to Carla. "They're back again then."

"Unfortunately," replied Carla. "I suppose you didn't speak to your husband?"

"I did actually. There's definitely change in the wind."

"Oh, no," said Carla.

"Don't start worrying yet. These things take ages. The whole thing will have to be just right. The last thing any of us want is for the tourist trade to be affected. We all aren't rich enough to own yachts. My husband said there's no need to panic. Anyway, I suppose there would be compensation."

"I just want to know what's going on." Carla replied doggedly and the two of them stood watching uncomfortably, until the roar of a sporty engine filled the street and parked under a palm tree by the paseo. Carla held her breath. Her mouth had gone quite dry.

Felipe jumped out and, without a glance in their direction, crossed straight over towards the knot of businessmen and surveyors. The men grinned as they shook hands.

"He's dishy, isn't he?" murmured Sancha. Carla didn't answer. She was thinking over the conversation she'd had with him. So he was involved. "If we had as much money as him, we wouldn't be worried." She spoke so familiarly, that Carla looked at her sharply.

"Do you know who he is?"

"I certainly do. That's Xavier Alvarez. Dona X's only son. The big boss. She owns all this and he acts for her. He's a lawyer."

"Her son?" cried Carla. And he wasn't called Felipe. Her heart plummeted. Maybe he'd mentioned Xavier as one of his eight names?

"Yes, why?"

"Oh, nothing," muttered Carla.

"You should ask *him* what's going on," said Sancha, "but we wouldn't get near him. His minders would see us off before you could say Quixote! Oh, well, it's all right for some. I'd better get on with the prescriptions. Bye." Sancha turned on her heel and disappeared into the cool darkness of the chemist's.

Carla could feel herself trembling all over. She was thinking how she'd confided in him; what he'd said about not wanting change on the island. And, all the time, he must have known exactly what was happening because he was the Dona's son and almost her landlord! She could feel her face burning, not only from embarrassment, but from sheer disappointment, that she had been taken in by his smooth talk.

She closed the shop and ran upstairs to her flat, imagining all kinds of things. He was probably trying to get on the right side of her, just so he could get hold of her business. He must think she was a fool. When was he going to come clean and tell her he knew exactly what was happening regarding the development? Perhaps he never would have!

She looked down through the window and stepped back behind the shutters in shock. Felipe was staring right across as if he was looking for her. She watched through a crack as he took out his mobile. A moment later, her phone rang. He was still looking up at the window.

Carla felt sick. She ignored the phone, ran across to her bedroom and threw herself down on the bed. Then, all the pent-up misery and disappointment of finding out that the first man she'd felt comfortable and safe with since Jack died was probably a fraud, welled-up and overflowed in a paroxysm of tears.

Finally, the phone stopped ringing.

Carla's eyelids were swollen with tears when she came to in that half-awake state between dream and reality. For a moment, she couldn't think why she felt so miserable, then she remembered! Groaning, she picked up her watch and peered into its unsympathetic face.

She couldn't believe it. She'd been asleep for four hours and as she stumbled across and opened half the shutters, a flaming red sunset was illuminating Santa Eulalia, setting both sea and houses on fire. She must have been tired. "More like totally worn out," she said.

After a hot cup of coffee, she felt more like herself. Why was she crying over a man she'd only just met? She should have more sense, she decided. Then she realised she was extremely hungry. She didn't want to think of the beautiful paella she'd enjoyed with him. What she needed at that moment was one of Kurt's pizza and chips and some human company.

She washed her face and brushed her hair, applied a slick of lipstick and hurried downstairs into the street. The Spanish were just coming alive, piling into restaurants to talk over the day's events. She was steering clear of the town centre and El Paso, which was Mercedes' haunt. No, Kurt's place was the answer. Elena was the place to go when you wanted cheering up.

She wandered down to the beach on the

way, which didn't do her a lot of good. It was the place where lovers went to look at the sunset, leaning on the ornate iron railings, staring at the sea and murmuring endearments; where families walked along happily, the children shouting and happy. Carla would have liked children, but now Jack had gone.

At that moment, things were looking black. Although she didn't want to, her feet were straying towards the yacht moorings. "You are not going to look for him, Carla," she said under her breath, but her feet kept on walking in that direction. "I shan't go right down there," she said.

The pontoon between the moored yachts was rough and sandy, and she made no noise as she approached. Music was floating on the air as she drew near to *La Paloma*. It was drowsy, soft and romantic.

Carla stopped and shrank back against one of the flagpoles. It felt wrong spying on him, but then she remembered all the things he'd said, which couldn't have been true. She had to look out for herself. Then she caught her breath.

A girl was hanging over the rail, looking out to sea, just as Carla had done after lunch. She had a gorgeous slim figure and dark, lustrous hair. Her dress was silver and slashed to the thigh and she was wearing the highest of high-heeled sandals.

Carla could hardly move as Felipe came out from the dining area. He was wearing a tuxedo and looked more handsome than ever. The girl was giggling as she turned to approach him. Carla gulped. There was no mistake. Felipe was entertaining Mercedes Carrea! And they were certainly more than business colleagues.

Carla closed her eyes momentarily at the double betrayal. That was where Mercedes must have been going when she met her a couple of nights ago walking towards the yacht harbour.

Turning abruptly, Carla hurried off. She'd seen more than enough for one day. Also her appetite seemed to have deserted her. All she wanted to do was go back to her flat and make some decisions about her immediate future.

5

"Do you know what I've decided to do?" asked Carla. She and Sancha were standing in the little cubby hole where the prescriptions were made up.

"What?"

"I've been thinking about it all night. About him!" replied Carla.

"I bet you have!" Sancha laughed. Carla wondered what the girl would say if she knew that Felipe and she had been out together; that he was the man she'd dressed up for.

"It's not like that. I'm going to see Dona X."

"You're what?" Sancha was astounded. "She won't agree to meet you. Her sort never does."

"She will, because I've phoned her already and I have an appointment in exactly three hours time. Eleven-thirty to be exact." Sancha looked amazed. "At least, then I might find out what's going on. My father used to tell me to go to the top if I needed anything and that's what I'm doing!"

"I've never heard of her having anything to do with her tenants personally." Sancha's mouth was still open.

"So? She's the one in charge and I need to know if I have wasted my very valuable investment," replied Carla firmly, although she didn't feel very tough at the moment, more like a quivering jelly inside.

"Good luck then," said Sancha admiringly. "You'll let me know the outcome, won't you?"

"Of course. Could you ask Martina to keep an eye on the shop for me?" She was the pharmacy assistant. "If she sees anyone really desperate to buy something," Carla grimaced, "get her to tell them I'll be open in the afternoon."

As Carla returned to her shop, she felt as though she had a weight on her shoulders, she couldn't shake off. She knew it was because of Felipe. She really had to forget him. Doubtless, as a lawyer, he'd come up with some explanation for his behaviour in not telling her who he was. But she wouldn't believe it. He had led her up the garden path.

The idea of speaking to his mother had

been a decision on the spur of the moment and she had been completely surprised at the reaction. It had been Dona X's secretary she had spoken to, who had promised to ring back and had been as good as her word, giving Carla precise instructions how to get to the villa.

The girl spoke very good English. "Dona Ximene will be very pleased to meet you. She asked me to tell you she desires to keep in touch with the small business people on the island. . . ." She continued then with the directions. "The Villa Cristina is quite easy to find, but it would be best to take a taxi as the road can be dangerous. However, should you wish to come by car . . . Have you a pen handy?"

Carla listened politely, but she didn't need to write anything down. The Villa Cristina was a house she was familiar with, on the outside at least, it was the place that she and Jack had found so appealing on their walks around the bay. Where else would a woman as rich as Dona X live? As for her son . . .

In spite of herself, Carla found herself imagining Felipe sitting on the terrace, surrounded by lustrous bougainvillea, his long legs stretched out, gazing over the horseshoe bay.

It must be paradise to live up there,

thought Carla. But he'd said he lived on the mainland now.

She felt a little flutter inside. Perhaps he'd be there when she called. That would give him a shock. Then she thought of him with Mercedes. They were probably lovers. Carla swallowed. What game was Mercedes playing? Saying she'd heard this and that. She must have known everything.

The taxi arrived on time, which was a surprise. Carla was wearing her suit for the first time since she'd come to Ibiza. It wasn't power dressing, but it made her feel efficient. She'd shied away from pure linen as it creased too easily. This one had a hint of another material, but only a hint. It was a warm beige tone, which Carla liked to think was so much more effective than the customary black, which always reminded her of funerals.

The only jewellery she was wearing were diamond studs in her ears. They had been Jack's last anniversary present to her. She felt he was beside her as she sat in the taxi and the driver began to negotiate his way out through the town's narrow streets.

But another image kept thrusting itself into her mind's eye. The man had deep dark eyes and high cheekbones. She could almost hear him whispering, "I like you a lot."

Carla steeled herself against any thought of Felipe as they crossed the river that gave its name to the town. They were using the new bridge, but she could see the much prettier old bridge below. According to local legend, the ancient one had been built by the Devil and it was said that many towns-folk wouldn't cross it at night. Carla smiled at the thought as the taxi raced through the hairpin bends into the open countryside.

They drove quickly past the smaller moun-tain on the top of which was the local church. What a climb that was, but it had been well worth it, when she and Jack had done it. Then Carla put the past out of her mind and concentrated on the future.

The taxi manouevred its way up into the hills surrounding the bay, until the road meandered into a leafy lane at the end of which stood the gate of the Villa Cristina. The arch that bore its name was fashioned from the local stone and from what you could see from the road, the villa itself had been constructed in the traditional rather than the modern style. That's why she and Jack had liked it, she thought, as she paid the driver and started up the steps.

She'd never believed on those early trips in the small hired car that she'd be climbing up to meet the owner. After one hundred steps, she was almost breathless and leaned on the wall for support wondering how on earth Dona X made it.

Then she knew, as the whole of the villa came into sight. There was another entrance reserved only for its inmates; a steep sloping road that snaked almost up to the front door. That wouldn't be nice if it was icy, she thought, forgetting she was on Ibiza where there wasn't much frost.

Three cars stood on the drive; a Land Cruiser, a black sporty-looking job — and then her heart almost stopped, a sleek sports with its nose poking out from behind the luxuriant bushes. Felipe was there!

At that moment, all she wanted to do was run back down the steps as quickly as she could. But Carla had never been a coward. Gathering together the last of her courage, she negotiated the last twenty steps and crossed the drive.

The view made her gasp. The Villa Cristina was a typical Ibicencan residence; thick-walled to keep out the heat with small windows on the front door side. But Carla knew they probably opened up widely inside, like the arrow slits used by archers in English castles. Such windows were put in to minimise the penetration of the sun's rays.

The whole villa lounged across the flat top of the mountain and the wonderful pool gushed down past her and lost itself over the shiny brown stones of a man-made waterfall. She could hear laughter coming from that direction. Maybe Felipe was in the pool? She dreaded the idea of being taken over there by a maid and having to talk to the family as they lounged about in their swimsuits like the stars in Hollywood films.

She was right about the maid, who must have been hovering near the door. "Buenos dias, senora." She wasn't young and beautiful, but getting on for sixty with the strong features of a peasant.

Carla was led into a cavelike room which was gloriously shady and entirely unpretentious. "I shall tell the Dona you are here," she announced. Relieved that she didn't have to go out to the pool, Carla stood uncertainly, then noticed the photographs which stood on a very expensive side table. Nearly all of them were of Felipe. The sight of him tugged at her heart.

"Good morning, Mrs Taylor." The lady's English was perfect. Like her son's, thought Carla. "Please sit down. I'm delighted to meet you." Dark eyes, so like Felipe's, probed Carla. The Dona had a young face, but her expression was sad rather than businesslike. Carla guessed she had seen much trouble. Of course, she was a widow and Carla knew what it was like to be both a widow and have business troubles.

The Dona was wearing a perfectly-tailored suit and silk blouse with an expensive brooch on the lapel and a single string of pearls round her neck. Carla was glad she'd opted for a suit too.

"Good morning, Mrs Alvarez," replied Carla, rather at a loss how to address her and wishing she'd taken more care thinking about it. She was definitely a real aristocrat, so should she have called her, 'My lady'. Too late now.

A moment later, Dona Ximene called for the maid. "Elise, would you bring in the coffee now and some ensaimadas? I hope you like our little specialities, Mrs Taylor?"

"Yes, please." Carla loved the local pastries and just had to have one, as did Dona X. Soon they were chatting away. Although Felipe's mother was the epitome of elegance as only the aristocratic Spanish can be, she was not haughty, but quite charming.

After more pleasantries, they began to talk about Carla's shop. There was no sign of Felipe or his companion, although occasional laughter and splashing could be heard. "Young people!" said the Dona, shaking her head. "Now, Mrs Taylor, please tell me why you have requested this meeting?"

Felipe's mother listened courteously to Carla's dilemma, only nodding her head now and again . . . "So you see, Mrs Alvarez, we — that is — the other shopkeepers and I are worried as we have no access to the plans. We're completely in the dark. You must appreciate that we would like to know where we stand."

"Nothing has been finalised yet," replied Dona X.

Carla breathed a sigh of relief, although she didn't like the word 'finalised'.

"I am still thinking about the harbour project," the lady went on. "I have not made up my mind whether to invest in the scheme or not. You see, it is not solely up to me. There are others involved. Of course, it is my land and you are my tenants, but I would wish to deal with you fairly.

"You may not know this, but I, too, have been the recipient of very high-handed treatment. As a young woman, my father accorded me no option but to take the worst land," she smiled, "— or so my family believed it to be — when he died, while the best, the fertile meadows of the interior went to my brothers. However, my late father was not a businessman, but a farmer. He had no idea that this island would become the centre of tourism and I, his only daughter, would reap all the benefits.

"Such a man he was." Her smile had a hint of mischief in it. "Luckily, he never knew my good fortune. I do respect women, who make their own way in the world without a man to guide them, although . . ." she shrugged, then rose from her chair. ". . . I have my son, who manages some of my legal business, but his ideas are not always compatible with mine."

I bet they're not, thought Carla miserably.

"I wish I could reassure you that you will not lose your shop, Mrs Taylor, but, at present, I cannot. It will be a joint decision, but I promise you that your compensation will be more than adequate should the scheme become operational."

"Oh, dear," said Carla, knowing remonstration was useless and that she was being dismissed. She could feel a pricking behind her eyelids and was horrified that she might break down or something silly like that. But a moment later, all thought of tears was forgotten, as the girl walked in.

"Oh, I'm sorry, Ximene, I didn't know you had a visitor," said Mercedes Carrea, stopping in consternation, then recovering herself. The lawyer was wearing a very brief bikini under a fluffy robe. "I'll go." Mercedes stared at Carla, who stared back in a very unfriendly manner. She was pretty sure she knew to whom the robe belonged!

"No, come and meet Mrs Taylor," said the Dona. "She's here to request some details of the harbour project."

"Miss Carrea and I have met already," replied Carla coldly. "Hello, Mercedes."

"That's wonderful. Then we are all friends," replied Felipe's mother, but Carla could see she was making a quick appraisal of the awkward situation. "Coffee, Mercedes? Cakes?"

"Why not?" asked Mercedes, who had regained her composure. Carla guessed that Felipe knew nothing about her being there either. Evidently, Dona X was close about her contacts.

"Mercedes is a good friend of my son's. By the way, where is Xavier?" Carla started at the unfamiliar name. Oh, yes, she thought, it must be one of the other eight! That's the one his mother uses too.

"He's getting dressed, Ximene." Carla could see Mercedes was very much at home and she was sure she knew why.

"Good. Perhaps you would like to stay and

meet Xavier, Mrs Taylor?"

"I would love to, but I'm afraid I can't. I have to open up the shop," replied Carla. No way was she going to wait to see him. "You've been very kind. And you have set my mind at rest for the moment," she lied.

Then her heart missed a beat as she heard footsteps behind her. She turned, but, unlike Mercedes, Felipe kept his cool. Although Carla was determined to hate him, her heart melted at the sympathetic and appealing look in his eyes, which she sensed was meant for her and only her, even though she didn't want to be the recipient of his pity.

"Well, Mother, entertaining guests without me?" Felipe looked stunning, his dark hair wet and his light cotton shirt open revealing luxuriant chest hair. His white shorts were fashionably long and his lithe brown legs were encased in fine Italian sandals.

Mercedes slid up from the chair and slipped her hand under his arm. "It's business, Xavier."

"Then I should have been here," he said, glancing at Carla, who held his gaze coolly.

"Darling, this is Mrs Taylor, who keeps a shop near the marina. She was worried about our plans. I think I have put her mind at rest."

"Good," said Felipe. "And good to meet you, of course, Mrs Taylor." He extended his hand and she had no option but to take it. Their eyes met again without a sign of open recognition.

"And you." She let go and looked at her watch. "I must call a taxi. May I go outside? I don't think I'll get a signal in here."

"No, no," interposed Felipe quickly. "I can take you back."

"Have you forgotten about our appointment?" reminded his mother. "I'm sorry, Mrs Taylor, but Xavier needs to be here."

"I can do it. Let me get changed," offered Mercedes.

"But I'd like you here too, dear," interposed Dona X. Mercedes flicked her a tiny smile.

"Thank you, but it won't take me long," insisted the girl. "I'll be back in time for the meeting. I promise." Carla gritted her teeth at such familiarity. She was determined to get rid of Mercedes as soon as possible. The last thing she wanted now was a two-timing solicitor.

"Please. I can easily call a taxi," she remonstrated, highly-embarrassed and more than annoyed.

"No. Mercedes will be delighted to help," said Dona Ximene. "We have to look after our tenants." Carla swallowed. Just what was going on?

"I'll go and put on something decent," said Mercedes, smiling at Felipe, who didn't respond and was frowning, his hands thrust in his pockets. As Mercedes made her exit, he turned to his mother and said, "I'll show Mrs Taylor the view from the terrace while she's waiting."

"Why not," asked Dona X. "It's very impressive." She looked at her son meaningfully.

As he ushered Carla across the room and outside, she was seething.

"What are you doing here?" he asked, when they were alone.

"How can you ask me that? You knew everything about the project and you wouldn't tell me," she accused.

"For a good reason," he hissed back.

"I don't want to hear," she said, turning away and staring miserably across at the view. He was so close to her that when the breeze tugged at her hair, it almost blew across his face. Carla shivered all over, although it wasn't cold.

"Believe me, Carla, I didn't want this to happen," he whispered. "For you to find out like this. I thought . . ."

"Don't try to explain," said Carla quietly.

"You're in league with Mercedes as well." She looked up at him. "She said she didn't know anything either. Do you both think I'm a fool? You lawyers may be smart but . . ."

"The last thing you are is a fool," he interrupted. "I'll explain everything soon."

"I think your mother has already done that," she retorted. "I don't want to see you again, Felipe. Or is it Xavier? I can't trust you."

"You can." The tone was sincere. "I promise you can." The affirmation was masterful. "I'll ring you."

"Don't bother," she snapped. A light step behind them proclaimed Mercedes's presence. She was wearing her black suit again and looked smartly impersonal, although her wet hair was glistening.

"Ready?"

"As I'll ever be," replied Carla bitterly. "You know I don't want to come with you."

"Don't be silly. It'll take ages to get a taxi at lunchtime. I don't mind dropping you off."

"Well, I do," hissed Carla. A moment later, they were joined by a calm Dona X, who began pointing out landmarks of interest to Carla. Unfortunately, Carla wasn't taking any of it in.

"Thank you again for your time, Mrs Alvarez," she repeated bleakly.

"I do hope we shall meet again," was the civil reply. Dona Ximene was either a very nice woman, or a good actor like her son. He was standing at a distance, wearing those inscrutable dark glasses.

"Goodbye, Mrs Taylor," he said.

"Goodbye." A bitterly-disappointed Carla nodded briefly in his direction and he gave an imperceptible little bow. Moments later, Carla was following Mercedes down the steps. "I don't want to go with you," she repeated.

"I don't think you are being very professional, Carla," remarked Mercedes briefly as they stood beside the car.

"What?" gasped Carla. "You knew all about the project and you still told me you knew nothing. You're supposed to be my lawyer and here you are, siding with the enemy."

"My private life has nothing to do with my work," said Mercedes, indicating the door. "I am attending the meeting precisely because I want to find out what's happening. Please get in."

Carla breathed in deeply and slammed the car door. Moments later, they were swinging down the mountain. This time the twisting of the road made Carla feel slightly sick.

Eventually, Mercedes said, "I'm sorry, Carla, but I'm engaged to Xavier. What do you expect me to do?"

"You're engaged to F . . . Xavier?" repeated Carla. She felt as if she was going to faint.

"Yes, almost."

"What does that mean?"

"He hasn't bought me a ring yet, but he will. He's a lovely guy. We get on so well."

"I'm sure you do. He's a good catch," replied Carla, grimacing.

"I shall ignore that. We are not like the English. A wedding is a matter for the families. Mine is delighted with the choice."

Carla wanted to blurt out, *Do you know he's two-timing you with me?* But she didn't. After all, it wasn't really true. It was all in her head.

"As for business," went on Mercedes, "naturally I know something of what goes on in the Alvarez household, but I am bound by confidentiality. However, as you have made it your business to come up here today and not take the advice I gave you to wait and see what happens, I can tell you that the car that just passed us was carrying Dona X's next appointment. Four of the other investors.

"I am not obliged to tell you anything, but I am trying to be fair. Xavier, who is an extremely powerful member of the group as Dona Alvarez's son, is in full agreement with the deal and, as his mother's legal representative, he has drawn up the documents for her to sign. I don't know what she told you today, but they are very near to agreement. My further advice to you is to take the compensation that will surely be offered. And if you wish to continue in business, you would probably find it more lucrative on the mainland. How about Barcelona?"

They didn't speak again until they were outside Carla's flat. "So what are you going to do," asked Mercedes.

"I'm considering my position, but I'm warning you that I shall probably be looking for a different legal representative," replied Carla coldly.

"That's your choice," said Mercedes. "I'm sorry it has ended like this."

"So am I," said Carla. "Thank you for bringing me home." She closed the door firmly and watched as Mercedes drove off.

A moment later, Sancha hurried out. "Well? What did Dona X say?"

"Not a lot, except that she has not made her mind up yet whether the project will go ahead. But I think the decision is imminent. She said there will be compensation."

Sancha shrugged. "Well, that's something."

"How can you be so calm? All my livelihood is tied up here." Carla looked at the shop.

"Que sera, sera," said Sancha.

"Thank you for that! See you," replied Carla and, putting the key in the lock, she slipped inside. A moment later, she sat down in her chair by the till and burst into tears.

Why am I crying? she asked herself for the hundredth time as she tried to comfort herself with some hot, sweet tea. Why did he pretend that he didn't know anything. Oh, he really took me in!

The whole afternoon and evening was one blot of misery. It was as if something had already been taken away from her, not only her shop, but something else too. She didn't want to wallow in self-pity, but she couldn't help it.

She'd tried so hard to build up the business — to follow her dream but, inside, it wasn't all about that. It was Felipe. He'd crept under the guard she'd put up when Jack died. And she'd believed he liked her for herself. She'd fallen into his trap. She was a fool in spite of what he said.

Anyway, she asked herself again, why are you even thinking about him. From now on, Felipe . . . Xavier . . . or whatever you're called . . . you're history. Pressing her lips together in a determined line, she sighed and went into the bedroom, which the sinking sun had filled with a lurid red light. Pulling across the shutters, she took off her clothes, lay down on the bed and snuggling into her pillows, switched on the television and watched a programme in which she had absolutely no interest at all . . .

Carla came to with a start. Her eyes felt swollen and she had a horrid sinking feeling in the pit of her stomach. At first, she couldn't remember what had gone wrong and when she did, she felt even worse. A look at her small alarm confirmed she'd slept until eight and the world was stirring outside.

But she didn't care. She was worn out. A couple of hours later, she had pulled herself together enough to venture out for a newspaper.

Buying one was a ritual. Carla had been taking Spanish lessons for some time and she always tried to avoid the day-old English papers and read a local one instead. Of course, one of her prime aims was to discover what was happening on the island and this morning that desire was even more pressing. Maybe there would be something about the harbour deal being struck?

"Don't be silly, Carla," she snorted out loud, as she tossed the hair out of her eyes and walked towards the kiosk, "this is Spain, for Heaven's sake. We'll probably never know until the bulldozers start tearing up the pavement!" Somehow, getting angry made her feel better, but she still couldn't stop glancing at the driver of every sports car that shot by.

"Hola," she said to the vendor, squinting up at the sky. It was going to be another wonderful day, which seemed so unfair, given the mood she was in. She only wanted to be happy, like the little family group that had just passed her going down to the shore, with the children jumping around with their brightly-coloured beach ball.

"Hola, senora," he replied with a grin, handing over her usual paper rolled-up. She knew he suspected she couldn't read it. She paid, then without looking at it, she walked behind the family towards the sea and the bordering avenue of gnarled and shady olive trees. It was a lovely place to sit and read at any time of the day.

She looked at her watch. "I don't think I'm going to open up. If you can't beat 'em, join 'em," she said ruefully. For her to make such a decision was unheard of, but, for some reason, and she knew very well what, she just didn't care to do anything she normally did.

She wanted to be just another holiday maker; to look at the sea like she did with Jack and not have all her present worries; to be a normal human being, not an anxiety-ridden business woman. It was all too much at the moment.

Carla sat down, unrolled the newspaper and gasped as she read the headline.

6

Right there! In front of Carla's eyes in bold print:

ISLAND'S PREMIER BUSINESSWOMAN INJURED.
SON A SUSPECT.

She couldn't believe it! Her eyes scanned the article, while the photographs of Dona X and Felipe smiled back at her. How could such a thing have happened?

Carla read on:

Elise, the maid, who had been with the family for many years, discovered her mistress lying unconscious at the foot of a flight of steps in the Villa Cristina.

There was no sign of an intruder and it is believed that Xavier, Dona Alvarez's only son, a lawyer from Madrid, was staying with his mother in the villa at the time. Senor Alvarez was nowhere to be found when the maid called for help. His bedroom was empty and his sports car was still parked in the driveway.

At first, it was suspected he might be injured too, but a search has revealed nothing. The police will not be drawn on the question that he may have been involved in some way for his mother's accident and that he had made a getaway by some other means.

Senor Alvarez owns a yacht, *La Paloma,* which is moored in the main harbour and which is presently under police surveillance. Meanwhile an island-wide search for him has been launched.

Carla put a hand to her forehead. It couldn't be true! Felipe would never do anything like that!

He wasn't the type. She knew he wasn't!

The article went on to say that the newspaper had it on good authority that Xavier Alvarez and his mother were at odds with a proposed development of the marina project and he had argued with her violently at an earlier meeting as to whether the project would go forward.

Several other photographs were inset; the German investors in the project, the ones that Carla had seen in the car, and there was even one of Mercedes Carrea, named as the suspect's girl friend.

Carla thought of what Mercedes had said; that Felipe was in complete agreement with them on the project. Could Dona X have decided against it then? It was a mystery.

"The poor woman," said Carla out loud. "It's absolutely terrible. But where's Felipe?" Then she panicked. Perhaps he'd been kidnapped or something. Even drowned? All kinds of horrible possibilities crowded into her mind. But not once did she even think he might have hurt his mother.

Carla closed the newspaper hurriedly, as another thought entered her head. Maybe the police would find out she'd been up to the Villa Cristina? In fact, she began to be sure they might interview her. Then it would come out she'd been seen with Felipe . . . Now her imagination began working over-time. By the time she got back to the shop, she was looking over her shoulder. Don't be foolish, she told herself, you've nothing to do with it anyway.

She had hardly walked into the door and gone upstairs when she heard the entry phone. "Who is it?" she asked.

"Sancha!" Carla relaxed.

"What's the matter?"

"Can I come up?"

"Of course."

Soon they were chatting about it over a cup of coffee with Carla doing her best not to give anything away about her involvement with Felipe, while Sancha made the most ridiculous suppositions. You don't know him like I do, Carla wanted to say, but she couldn't.

"Anyway, why aren't you open?" asked Sancha.

"I felt a bit lazy — and upset, I suppose."

"By what's happened?" Sancha looked extremely interested.

"No, I feel uptight. I can't settle to anything with the thought I might lose my business," lied Carla, although the lie was half-true. Sancha seemed quite satisfied with the explanation and eventually disappeared.

In spite of her earlier decision, Carla thought it would be sensible to open the shop after all, given what was happening and the afternoon passed quietly enough with about a dozen sales, which meant that summer was on its way and the tourists were returning. But when Carla decided to go down to Kurt's bar, Elena, to fetch a chicken sandwich, the tongues of the local population were only wagging about one thing; Dona X's accident.

"That was her son you were talking to in

here, you know," said Kurt pointedly.

"Pardon?" Carla's heart skipped a beat.

"That good-looking guy. Don't tell me you don't remember!" Kurt grinned.

"When?"

"Last time you were in. He was chatting you up."

"Him?" Carla feigned utter surprise. "He's Dona Alvarez's son? You're kidding me. I wish I'd known." She gave a good imitation of a laugh.

"You would have then, if you'd known how rich he was, but not now. I reckon he might have done it!" Then someone interrupted with the opposite opinion. Carla listened carefully. Most of the locals seemed to have nothing to say but good about Felipe.

He'd evidently been a popular boy in the town; generous and clever. "He was never one of the elite," declared one of his defenders. "Always had a kind word. Stopped to talk. Never forgot his roots. He works for his living. He doesn't sit round all day like some of the people on the yachts. He's a proper gentleman."

Carla's heart felt lighter. It seemed as if she'd forgotten what he'd made her feel when he hid his identity from her. He'd said he would explain. Now she knew it was very unlikely she'd ever hear that explanation.

Half an hour later, Carla left the bar, her mind in a turmoil. She wandered through the harbour and found her steps were carrying her towards Felipe's yacht. She caught her breath as she saw the uniformed policeman, lighting a cigarette on the quay. The newspaper report was true on that score. They evidently were keeping an eye on *La Paloma*.

Carla's eyes filled with tears. Such an awful thing to happen in such a lovely place. She'd thought Dona X had been very reasonable the way she'd treated her and the thought that Felipe might hurt his mother made Carla shiver. She shook her head. Although she'd known him for a very short time, she decided she really couldn't believe it.

Someone else must have been responsible for the accident. Dona X probably slipped. The place was full of awkward steps. But, then, why had Felipe disappeared? It was no good trying to guess. She breathed in deeply, turned quickly away and headed back for the flat.

A strong night wind blew over the dark sea and bent the palm trees on the front, making the fairy lights strung between their branches toss pinpricks of coloured light across the bay. In the marina, the yachts pulled at their ropes like tethered horses, eager to be free.

Carla hadn't gone for her usual evening walk along the paseo. Instead, she'd stayed at home and read the account in the newspaper so many times she almost knew it off by heart. She'd also stared at his photo endlessly. She felt as if she was involved in the matter, which was quite ridiculous. What was she to him anyway? A passing acquaintance? But her heart had been telling her otherwise, even since she met him.

She made a half-hearted attempt to clear up the living room, which she'd been neglecting and, when she'd finished, switched on the local television news. The Alvarez story wasn't local any more. It had gone national. Felipe was a wanted man.

He was a lawyer. Why would he want to run away? She gasped when she saw the footage. Merecedes's familiar face was filling the screen as she hurried away, accompanied by her own lawyer. Evidently she must have had something to say about the attack. Perhaps they thought she knew where he was? After all, she was described as his girlfriend.

Carla lay back in her chair, but she couldn't relax. She was too jumpy. Sighing, she got up and went into the kitchen. Then she heard the buzz of the entry phone and looked at her watch. Ten o' clock. She gulped. Perhaps it was the police? But why should it be? She'd done nothing. But you were at the villa on the day, mocked a nasty little voice in her head. She picked up the phone gingerly, "Who is it?"

"Felipe. Please, open the door." Carla gasped. She couldn't believe it. What did he want? "Please, Carla, will you let me in?" It was now or never. Whose side was she on? He could be dangerous, said the mean small voice of her reason. But her heart was telling her otherwise.

"All right. Come up." She pressed the buzzer and stood shaking. What have you done, Carla, she asked herself. A moment later, he was knocking. Breathing in deeply to calm herself, she opened the door, which was still on the chain. "What do you want?" she whispered.

His face was strained and pale. He didn't look sophisticated or supremely in charge; he seemed just an ordinary guy in an open-necked white shirt and blue jeans. He looked broken. His hair was rumpled from the wind and Carla felt a sudden jerk of sympathy for him that almost tore her apart. He couldn't have hurt his mother!

"I need to explain," he said. She noticed he was carrying a briefcase. She slid back the chain and let him in. "Thank you," he replied, looking round. "Thank you so much." His dark eyes glistened with emotion. "May I sit down?" She gestured the couch and sat down opposite him. "First of all, I want you to know," he added, "I would never harm my mother!"

"I know," she said, simply. He looked startled, then relieved.

"Do you? I hardly . . ." He broke off and she sensed why.

"You hardly know me," Carla finished the sentence for him. He didn't answer. "Why did you come to me, Felipe?" She wanted to hear him say it.

"I felt that you might understand. And . . . I didn't know where else to go," he said, looking across at her. "I need your help." Carla's heart lurched in her chest. "I have no right to ask — to get you involved. I came because I think of you as a friend, in spite of how you feel about me. Please believe me that I didn't want to deceive you. I was going to tell you that I was her son . . ." He gestured helplessly and put his hand over his eyes.

"How badly hurt is she?" asked Carla quietly.

"She's unconscious and I can't even go to see her." Suddenly, his dark eyes flashed. "They'll pay for this!"

"Who will?"

"Our enemies. I've been . . . framed, Carla? Is that the right word?" She nodded.

"Yes, but not one I've ever experienced. Why would anyone want to frame you, Felipe?"

"Because I am against this idea of pulling the island to pieces," he retorted. "My island!" The old touch of arrogance returned. She would have smiled if things hadn't been so serious. He didn't own it all.

"I want it to . . ." he added, shrugging, ". . . to stay more or less as it is now. We have enough tourism. Of course we must progress, but we do not have to rip the place to pieces. These men . . . I'm sorry . . . I'm not explaining very well . . ."

"You mean these men did this to your mother because you persuaded her not to sign — and then blamed you for it? Who are they?"

"They call themselves international businessmen but, in reality, they are nothing more than puppets, who are backed by thugs! I tried to tell her in the beginning about their background. I have been researching them for some time. That's why I came over in a hurry.

"My mother is very strong-minded. She thought it would be good for us all but, in this case, she was wrong. I knew I could persuade her to take another path. But they intended otherwise. And this was the way they found to force our hands. Those men will stop at nothing. I believe they have said that they can produce the contract signed by my mother? It must be forged. I can't bear to think that they forced her to sign and then . . . !" Felipe jumped up, his lips set and white. He was really worked up now. "They would stop at nothing. Even murder."

Carla breathed in deeply. It sounded plausible, but she had to ask. "Where were you when it all happened, Felipe? They said your car was there, but you weren't?" She stared at him and he returned her gaze steadily.

"I was with Mercedes."

"I see." A wave of disappointment rolled over Carla, then dissipated. "Well, that's good news," she said quietly. "She'll give you an alibi."

"That's the problem," he said. "She will not! In fact, she has already told the police

I was not with her."

"What? Why?"

"That I find difficult to tell you at present. All I can say is that I am sure she knew what was going to happen to Mother, because she insisted I come back with her to her place, before it happened. She said she had some alternative plans that I'd like to see. Some documents. And like a fool, I believed her. The whole thing must have been planned."

His face shut down like a cold mask. "Do you believe me, Carla?" He walked over to her and put his two hands on her shoulders. "She will not give me an alibi and I have to make her!"

"How?" asked Carla, her voice trembling a little.

"With your help. You are the only person I can turn to." In other circumstances, the words might have been a compliment. But here he was, asking her to help him make his girlfriend swear she was with him while a crime was being committed. How did he think Carla felt about that? "Will you help me?" His breath was warm on her face and his eyes were pleading. "Will you do this for me?"

"I . . . I'm not sure."

"I understand," he said, turning away. "I

had no right to ask but . . ." he stopped. Her woman's instincts told her what he wanted to say, that she meant something to him.

She put out her hand and laid it on his arm. "I didn't say I wouldn't help. It's just that . . ." She caught her breath.

"You can't trust me?" A spark of hope lit up his eyes. "You can, Carla. I promise you can."

"You said that before, Felipe."

"I know — and I meant it. And I mean it again."

Carla stood uncertain how to proceed and he must have caught her look, sensed her doubts, because he was staring at her. "No! This is very wrong of me. I can't ask you to get involved. I should be going now."

"Don't!" said Carla suddenly. "I'll help you, Felipe. But I need to know the facts. Sit down. You look like you could use some coffee." She saw the utter relief in his eyes as he slumped back in the chair and passed a hand over his forehead.

Carla walked into the kitchen and, as she switched on the percolator, she murmured under her breath, "Well, you've done it now, girl. You're in it up to the neck. You've only yourself to blame!"

7

The paseo was deserted as Carla walked nonchalantly along under the fairy lights. She was trying not to think of how Felipe had slipped into the sea and was now swimming around the rocky breakwater to reach *La Paloma* and steal his own inflatable with the outboard motor.

What she did want to think about, was how they'd walked in the dark across the sand, which was still warm under their feet, their arms around each other, like lovers. How they sat down on the sand so he could change into his wet suit, so he only looked like someone going for a night swim and would escape the notice of anyone who was watching from the seaside flats or a parked car.

He'd asked her to sit there for a short time, before she carried on with the plan they had made and, during those anxious few minutes, she'd tired of staring at the black water for a sight of him and looked up instead into the inky moonless sky, which was strewn with brilliant stars, imagining that nothing awful had happened and they were only a couple in love enjoying time together.

She still wasn't sure why she'd agreed to to distract any watching policeman so that Felipe could take the small boat that trailed behind *La Paloma* without being caught. Nor even if she was cool enough to pull it off.

"Won't they hear the engine?" she'd asked, when he'd explained.

"I'll row the inflatable and I won't start up the motor until after I've picked you up by the breakwater," he said.

When Carla reached Kurt's place, her heart was beating very quickly. It accelerated even more when she saw the two policemen standing outside, sipping what looked like glasses of beer. They were laughing and joking, but their guns were well in evidence.

She walked past them, conscious of their glances and halted to look into a brightly-illuminated shop window, which sold a range of fishing tackle and boat equipment. She swallowed as one of them approached.

"Senorita? You're out late. And alone?"

He grinned, showing perfect white teeth.

"Yes, I'm waiting for my boyfriend," she lied. "He's picking me up round the corner. Then we're going clubbing." She smiled in a very friendly manner as the other policeman joined them.

"Lucky lad," said the first, looking at his watch. "Is he Spanish?"

"No, he's from London. Why?" asked Carla.

"Thought so. We wouldn't want one of our girls wandering round here at night, would we?" The other shook his head.

"Why? Are you offering to escort me then?" asked Carla cheekily, her heart thudding in her ears as she thought of Felipe untying the inflatable and rowing it away.

"We'd love to, but we're on duty," said the second, leering at her.

"Is something going on? Is that why you're here?" asked Carla innocently. She couldn't believe how good she was at deceit.

"Yes, we're keeping an eye on the yachts. And we'll get in trouble for talking to you, if our boss comes round."

"You poor things! You've worried me now," she said sweetly. "Are you sure you wouldn't like to walk to the corner with me?" They stared at her and she wondered if she'd gone too far and what was a Spanish prison like!

"I don't see why not," said the other. He looked extremely interested. Too much, in fact.

"You can't. We have to stay here." They began to argue.

"That's all right," snapped Carla and flounced off, her high heels tap-tapping on the pavement. She hadn't wanted to get dressed-up, but Felipe had pointed out she couldn't go clubbing in a fleece!

"My boyfriend wouldn't have liked it anyway," she called. "Bye!" She could feel their eyes watching her all the way round the corner. At least they weren't taking any notice of the yachts. She could feel the perspiration running down her forehead. That had been playing with fire. She couldn't believe what she'd done.

When she felt she'd got away far enough, she consulted her watch. He'd said he estimated it would take around twenty minutes rowing before he reached the breakwater on the far side of the marina. Carla shivered and kept glancing back. Had he managed to pull it off?

She walked on and stood by the wall looking out to sea, praying that the policemen wouldn't check on her. Ten minutes passed, as well as a couple of pedestrians, who stared at her curiously. Feeling both awkward and a little afraid, she pulled her shrug about her shoulders and leaned against the hard stones. Then, a moment later, a voice hissed, "Carla? I'm here." She gasped with relief and hurried down the steps onto the beach. A dark shape approached.

"Felipe. Thank goodness. It's half an hour since you went. I was afraid you'd drowned."

"Don't worry, I'm used to these waters," he said. "I've been swimming in these currents since I was that high!" He gestured. "Come on then. We have to go before they realise the inflatable's gone."

A few moments later, Carla was seated in the boat and Felipe was rowing strongly out to sea. She gasped as the waves hit the sides with force, but Felipe didn't stop paddling. She thought then how strong he was! Once they were well away from the shore, he started up the powerful motor.

"Are you okay?" he asked. She couldn't see his expression, but she heard the anxiety in his tone. "Come over," he said. "Carefully! You can sit here by me, while I use the rudder. And slip this on. You're shivering." He handed her a substantial anorak. "I've another wet suit," he gestured. "You can put that on later."

"I'm not swimming," she protested.

"I don't want you to, but you'll be better protected when we get where we're going."

"Which is?"

"Better not to know at present," he replied. "I won't do anything terrible, I promise you. All I want is a witness . . ." he stopped, ". . . No, not quite that. Among other things, I mean." She felt him slip his free hand around her waist and draw her to him. Then he kissed her on the cheek. "Thank you for this, Carla. I'll be forever in your debt." She tried to laugh it off, but she could still feel his kiss burning her, as the moon suddenly came out. "Thank God that didn't happen when I was taking the boat," he added.

They gazed at each other. "You're beautiful in the moonlight," he said, his eyes only dark holes above his high cheek bones.

"You're not too bad yourself," she said, to lighten the intenseness of the atmosphere. The whole thing was surreal. She was seated in a boat with a handsome guy who looked like James Bond dressed in a black wet suit and they were bound for an unknown destination. Things like that didn't happen to Carla Taylor! But now they were.

She wondered how she'd cope when they reached where they were heading. He'd explained that he intended to make Mercedes withdraw her statement to the police.

"Just how do you expect to do that?" she'd asked.

"Quite easily," he said, indicating the briefcase that now lay on the bottom of the boat. It was encased in a waterproof bag . . . They were both lost in their own thoughts as they skimmed over the water, the bow of the powerful inflatable scorching through the glassy surface.

"We're nearly there," he said. They had left the horseshoe bay of Santa Eulalia and were approaching the lights of what Carla thought was Es Canar, a neighbouring village. But they passed it and rounded a desolate headland, until they saw a single cluster of lights above the shoreline. "I'm cutting the engine," he said. "That's the Villa Carrea above."

A moment later, silence overcame them. Carla sat listening to the plish-plash of the oars as he steered into the small bay at the end of which was a low, white-plastered building. She panicked for a moment, then recovered herself. A moment later, the inflatable juddered on the beach. They jumped out and Felipe dragged it round the side of the boathouse with her help.

"That's where Mercedes keeps her boat,"

he said. "Now, we're going to climb up there." He pointed up a thin string of white path. "I want you to put on the wet suit now. I won't look at you, only at the villa." He produced a pair of binoculars and turned his head while she struggled into it.

"Ready," she said, grimacing at what she must look like.

"You look good," he added, as if he was reading her thoughts. Then he picked up a small knapsack. "Look in here. The player and the phone. Ok?"

"Fine. Let me put my bag in too." He watched as she pushed in the small leather bag she'd been wearing. "I'm not leaving it in the inflatable," she said. He smiled and shook his head. She knew he was thinking, Women and their handbags! She slipped on the light knapsack. "Ready. How are you going to get in the house?" she asked, her stomach doing somersaults.

"I have a key." Of course he had!

"Does anyone else live there?"

"No. Mercedes prefers to be alone. She likes to do her own thing. It's only a small villa."

"How do you know she's in?"

"I saw the car." They walked quietly up the sandy path, then Felipe said, "That's the terrace." She looked. "I'm going to go round the front and . . ." he paused and drew her to him, ". . . and I want you to walk up to the terrace. It's all right. She has the curtains drawn at present." Carla opened her mouth to remonstrate. How was she going to see anything?

"I know I shouldn't be asking you to do this, but . . ." he added, "you're the only person I can rely on. Nothing's going to happen to you. I would like you to walk up there quietly and stand behind that big flowering bush by the patio windows. I'm going to draw Mercedes into your view. I want you to use this." He withdrew the MP3 player and a sophisticated mobile phone, which he handed over. "You have to record our conversation," he said. "And, if possible, get some pictures for evidence."

"I don't know if I can do it, Felipe," she said.

"Why?" His eyes probed her face.

"Scared, I suppose. And worried."

"I know. I'm begging you, Carla. This is the only way she'll see sense. I am not going to take the rap for my mother. Neither is Mercedes going to lie about me. Will you help me, please."

"I'll try but," she looked round. "I don't know how I agreed to this. Nor why. And I don't know how you're going to get her to change her mind."

"Leave that to me," he said. "You're a good person, Carla, and you want to see justice done, don't you?"

"Of course but . . ." She shrugged helplessly.

"If I tell you why I really asked you to help, you mightn't believe me now." Her stomach turned. "That's why I haven't. But I suppose I should take that chance."

"I don't understand."

"The chance you won't believe me. I'm going to try though. All I know is, there's something between us that . . ." He hesitated, then began again. "Something I've never felt before with a woman. I can't explain that something, because you'll think I'm trying to manipulate you. I'm not. I truly feel it. I did from the moment I saw you."

"What did you feel?" she asked wildly. He ignored the question.

"You know why I came into your shop?"

"To suss out the place?"

"No! I wanted to make your acquaintance and when you told me later how upset you were by not knowing what was going to happen with your shop, I felt I couldn't reveal that I was her son. I wanted to dissuade my mother from signing the documents, so that

I could . . ." He stopped.

"Could . . .?" encouraged Carla.

"Take you to meet her — or something like that. You've got right under my skin, Carla. I want you. Don't you understand?" Her head whirled for a moment, but she recovered herself.

"Where does Mercedes fit in? She said you were engaged."

"Nowhere. She's the last person I want to marry. I don't trust her. I never have."

"So why was she up at the villa? Why was she so familiar with you and your mother?"

"I've known her since we were kids. We went to school together. Her father and my father always wanted . . . You know what I mean. But I didn't, and she couldn't bear it. Especially when I told her I was seeing someone else." Carla's heart went into overdrive. "Yes, I told her about the new woman I'd met. And she didn't like it. In fact, she was so mad, she decided to drop me right in it. She even tried to blackmail me. But she's not going to get away with it. Why are you looking like that?"

"It's all too much. I . . . I can't take in what you're saying. We've only just met!"

"Yes, we have, but I know you feel the same, else why would you be doing this for me?" They stood breathing heavily in the dark, the wind blowing their hair. "I hope you believe me. Carla, you do, don't you?"

"I want to," she said in a small voice.

"I swear I'm not saying this, only because I want your help." His voice was urgent. She had to say something.

"Okay, I'll do it."

"Thank you!" She heard the relief in his voice. Carla shook back her hair and said, "So — you want me to climb up there?"

"Yes, I'll watch you get into position before I go in."

"And then?"

"After I'm inside, I'll get her out on to the terrace."

"What?" Carla nearly shrieked.

"Don't worry. I know what I'm doing. She'll be too busy with me to notice you."

"It's too risky!" Carla's voice shook.

"Trust me. When we go back in, you go back down to the inflatable and wait for me. Now, are you sure you know how to use these?"

"Yes," said Carla. She was used to the MP3. "Felipe, what if anything goes wrong?"

"It won't!" He looked at his watch. "We better get going."

"This is illegal, isn't it?"

"Legally, no conversation should be recorded without the other person knowing, but this is a special case. If anything did happen, then I'll say I made you do it. But it won't," he repeated. "Ready?"

As she climbed up towards the terrace, Carla was really scared. She asked herself over and over again what she was doing spying on someone. Especially a lawyer.

The bush was enormous, thrusting out on to the terrace. Felipe knew what he was doing, because if you parted it a little you could get a wonderful view of the steps down from the window. But you could hear the sea below and she was afraid that might affect the recording. Her heart was in her mouth as she settled herself. She could hear music inside the villa. He'll have to remember to get that switched off, she thought.

He was standing below watching her. Then she saw him take off the wet suit and get dressed. Finally, he took out the brief-case. A moment later, he was springing up the steps and round the building.

Carla's heart was beating much too quickly as she got his equipment out. She hoped she was going to be able to do it. She took out her own MP3 and mobile as well. Just in case. Somewhere inside the door bell rang. Then the music was switched off and she could hear voices.

She nearly collapsed when she heard the patio doors slide open, and the light from inside, flood the terrace. It seemed an age until she could actually hear their conversation and then she froze as the two of them stepped out.

Mercedes was wearing a robe, which did little to disguise her figure. She'd evidently been in bed!

"It's cold," she said. "Let's go in." Carla gasped and switched on.

"I want you to see something," he said. "I came all this way by boat at this time of night to talk to you." Carla could see he'd positioned them for the best view. "That's how much I needed to see you."

"I'm not going to change my story." Mercedes shook her head, her face full on to the mobile. That's going to be a lot of help, thought Carla. Her fingers were shaking so much she was afraid she'd drop the things.

"That's exactly what your statement was. A story!" said Felipe. "Why do you hate me so much, Mercedes? You can't make someone love you." The girl pouted.

"I'd like to slap your face," she snarled. "How could you go out with that . . ." Carla stiffened.

"I'd like you to do that," he said, "rather than perjure yourself!" You're so clever, thought Carla. He's trying to provoke. "You know what the penalty is — because when my mother comes round, she'll know who did it."

"Maybe she won't come round?"

"Do you want that, Mercedes?"

"Of course not!"

"Do you want me to lie to you? Say I love you when I don't. We've been friends for a long time."

"I want to be more than friends with you, Felipe." Carla could hear the desperation in the girl's voice and gritted her teeth as Mercedes tried to snuggle into Felipe's arms. "If only . . ."

"If only you'd say that you loved me; that we'd get engaged, I'd retract the statement."

"Would you?" he asked calmly. "You'd still be up for perjury."

"I could say I was scared of them. That they'd do the same to me." Her voice was louder and Carla felt triumphant. They had her now.

"Which you are. How much did they say they'd pay you to lie?"

Mercedes shrugged." "It wasn't the money!"

"So they did offer you money then."

"All right, but it wasn't the cash!" repeated Mercedes. "I didn't care about that. It was . . . Oh, Felipe, if you'd only say you love me." She was hanging on to his arm.

"I can't do that," reorted Felipe, shaking her off, "because it isn't true. I love someone else."

"You ba . . ." Mercedes put up her hand to strike him, but he held her off. "I love you!"

"How can you even say you love me, if you want to see me suffer. To frame me. You know I was with you. You saw to that."

"Only hold me, tell me you care and I'll give you your alibi!" She was clinging on to him. "I wanted you to stay the whole night and you wouldn't."

Carla was perspiring freely now, and not only because she was dressed in the wet suit. They had their evidence, so why didn't he finish and go inside. She couldn't bear much more.

"If I stayed with you tonight, would you tell the police that you were lying." Mercedes nodded. Carla was gasping silently. "Say it then! At least, own up to me."

"If you stay, I'll tell them the truth. That you were with me all afternoon and evening!"

"Thank you," said Felipe. "Well, I'm sorry to disappoint you, Mercedes, but I'm prepared to take my chances with the law. Do you think I'd stoop to staying with a woman who'd betray me for her own ends?" He laughed bitterly. "I bet you didn't know that in that briefcase were some documents I'd drawn up to offer you a partnership if you were willing to tell the truth. But we won't need them now, will we?"

Carla blinked at the evil look on Mercedes's face.

"I hate you," the girl screamed. "I hope you go to prison!"

"For a crime I didn't commit?"

"Yes!" she shouted. "You can go to Hell, for all I care."

"The feeling's mutual," retorted Felipe. "I'll get going now, shall I!" He turned on his heel.

Mercedes shot inside after him and Carla almost collapsed. She clicked off the MP3s and closed the phones. Now she had to make her getaway. Was it safe?

Breathing a silent prayer, she stole off down the path and made for the boathouse. She kept in the shadows as much as possible, just in case Mercedes was watching for the inflatable to leave then, once she was the other side of the boathouse, she sat and checked the recordings and photos. It was all there. She put them on the seat. Then she looked at her own.

117

Her phone pics weren't too bad either for a small mobile. Certainly good enough to nail Mercedes if they hadn't had the others! Carla put her own phone and player carefully into the knapsack and changed back into her own clothes. Then she put on the anorak again, because the night wind was definitely cutting after the warmth of the wet suit.

The minutes seemed interminable until Felipe appeared. "Did you get it?" he asked. She nodded and handed him over his equipment. "I've looked at it and listened to the recording. Well, some of it!" He knew what she meant. That she wasn't keen on hearing his conversation with Mercedes again. He still spent a few minutes checking the evidence. Just like a lawyer!

"Well done!" He put the player and mobile in his briefcase. A moment later, he was kissing her. "Thank you for everything. I'll make it up to you in any way I can!" She didn't reply, only helped him drag out the boat. Then he started up the motor.

"She'll hear that."

"I couldn't care less," he said. "She's probably phoning the police right now. Or maybe she's crying into her pillow."

"You were brutal," said Carla.

"She deserved it," he said. Carla didn't

respond. A few seconds passed, then he added, "Everything I said was true, you know."

"About?"

"About me loving someone else. You."

"How can you say that?" Her heart was thudding.

"I can say it, because I am one hundred per cent sure. I told you, I've never felt like this with anyone else." She shook her head wordlessly.

"What will happen now?" she asked, afraid that nothing would work out after all.

"I'll drop you off, then I'll go to the yacht and wait for them."

"I'll wait with you."

"No, I don't want you to be involved in this sordid mess."

"I couldn't be more involved," she remonstrated. He let go of the rudder with one hand and stretched out the other.

"Come here," he said. "Thank you, my darling, for all you did tonight. But I want you to go home. I'll wait and see if I have to reveal my sources. I could have taken anyone to the villa to be my witness. Why do they have to know it's you?"

"Please, Felipe, let me help. Say they don't believe you."

"They will," he said. "And if they don't,

then I'll tell them where to come."

Carla lay with her head against his shoulder, looking up at the starlit sky, while the inflatable sped through the waves. It seemed so much quicker returning than it had when they set off.

As the lights in the bay drew nearer, he cut the engine. "I've made up my mind," she said. He turned to look at her.

"What about?"

"I'm coming with you to the yacht."

"No, you're not."

"I am," she persisted. "If I could do what I've done, I think I'm entitled to see the whole thing through." He stared at her. "Anyway, I want to be with you when you face the police."

"You may get into trouble," he said.

"It doesn't matter. We're in this together." Carla knew she was taking a risk, but she only had to look at his face to know what she was doing was right. He sighed and stared across at the harbour.

"You might find yourself in the cells."

"Well, I'll ask for the British Consul."

"And you think that will help?"

"I told you, I want to do this. I want to be with you."

"I want that too . . ." He shrugged helplessly.

"Well, let's get on with it then. In for a penny, in for a pound?" She saw his puzzled look. "An old English saying. I won't explain." She sat back as if he she hadn't a care in the world. He leaned over and kissed her.

"All right, as I can't get rid of you, here goes." He picked up the oars and started rowing towards the harbour. The moon was out as the inflatable slipped in between the rocky breakwater with its look-out tower on the point.

They glided noiselessly along the row of yachts. If there were still policemen watching, then neither of them could be seen. Felipe tied up the inflatable and helped Carla on to the ladder, which was positioned on *La Paloma*'s white side. He handed her bag over and she began to pull herself up with him following her.

She was concentrating so hard that she remembered just as she reached the platform step, but he was already beside her, holding his briefcase. She looked over her shoulder, hanging on to the rope handles. "I've left something behind." How could she have forgotten? "My MP3 player and phone! I left them in your knapsack!"

"Don't worry. Nobody's going to steal them from my inflatable, are they?" She grimaced.

"I suppose not, but . . ." It would be awful if somebody did, especially since they might need the duplicated evidence. "But . . ." she shrugged, ". . . But I suppose they'll be fine."

"All right, I'll go back for them in a minute, but let's have a drink first." They stared through the windows of the saloon. "The police have turned the place over," he said grimly. "Okay, let's go inside."

"I need the bathroom," she murmured. But she never got there. As they walked through, the door slammed behind them and Carla screamed as she felt something hard pressing into her back. She had no option but to move, until she was pressed, face to the bulkhead. Then someone turned her roughly.

"Welcome," said the man, who stood in front of them. A black balaclava hid his face and he wore a black polo neck and trousers. The two men with him were dressed exactly the same. Each was holding a pistol. "We've been waiting for you, senor, but we didn't expect you to have a new girlfriend in tow!"

Carla shot a frightened glance at Felipe, who was struggling as his arms were being twisted behind his back. The look in his eyes clearly said, *I'm sorry, Carla, that I got you into this. Will you forgive me?*

The three of them had been waiting for Felipe to turn up. How they got past the police, Carla didn't know. Instead, she and Felipe were forced to watch as the man in charge went through his briefcase.

The look on Felipe's face was sickening, when the leader found the evidence. Then man chuckled as he listened and looked at the photos. "Well, lads, we're lucky," he grinned, handing the phone round. "The boss is going to be delighted."

"Who's the boss?" asked Felipe.

"Wouldn't you like to know," the man retorted.

"Were you the one who hurt my mother?" Felipe asked bravely and was rewarded by a kick. He cried out in pain.

"Felipe!" cried Carla, but she couldn't go to him. "Don't say any more, please!"

"She's being sensible," said the man. "It might be dangerous for both of you. In fact . . ." he considered, "just what am I going to do with you?"

"You could hand us over to the police," said Felipe recklessly.

"I don't think so," he said, indicating the evidence. "There's only one place for these!" He picked up the MP3 player and mobile and handed it to one of the other men. "Get rid of it!"

The man went outside and returned a few moments later. "They're in the drink," he said.

"Now, you," said the man-in-charge, turning to Carla. She watched as the man turned out her bag and sorted through her things. It sickened her to think he'd touched everything that belonged to her. Felipe's face was white and grim, but all Carla could think of was if they searched the inflatable, they'd find the knapsack!

After the bag, they frisked her. But she got through it somehow by gritting her teeth and closing her eyes, because she couldn't bear the helpless look on Felipe's face. When the search was over, they grinned. "She's clean!"

Then the two of them dragged Felipe across the floor towards her and pushed him against the bulkhead. "Sit there and be quiet both of you." Next moment, the two left and stood talking with the other outside on the companionway. Neither Carla nor Felipe could hear.

"What do you think is going to happen?" she whispered.

"I don't know. They're probably deciding right now. I'm so sorry I got you into this," he said, miserably.

"Don't be!" She was trying to be brave, but she was really terrified.

"There's still hope. Mercedes probably phoned the police, after we went. If their brains are working, they'll be down here double quick. Not that it'll do me much good," he groaned. She wanted to tell him about the duplicate evidence, but thought better of it. It might be bad luck. And the men still didn't come back.

"Do you think they've gone?" she said, after what seemed an age.

"Well, they got more than they came for," he replied bitterly, his head bowed.

"Not quite," said Carla. "As long as they didn't leave in the inflatable!"

"What do you mean?" he asked.

"I mean . . . I duplicated the evidence. It's in the knapsack. Under the seat." He stared at her uncomprehendingly. "My own MP3 and my mobile. I recorded the conversation between you and Mercedes on mine."

"You blessed girl," he gasped. He was trying to twist his hands free, but it was hopeless. He leaned towards her and toppled over.

"Don't, please. What are you doing?" She couldn't help him, as he struggled upright breathlessly.

"I was trying to kiss you." She smiled at him through a haze of tears. Then sirens began to wail somewhere in the distance.

8

The night following the adventure was tough for both of them, but especially Felipe. They were questioned separately. The policeman who interviewed Carla was curt. He tried to catch her out.

"Why did you go to Miss Carrea's house?"

"I've told you already," she said. "I went with Mr Alvarez to prove his innocence."

"You were trespassing. According to Miss Carrea, you entered private property."

"Well, I didn't know that at the time. Anyway, Mr Alvarez used his own key. I never went inside. He asked me to be a witness to his conversation." She was getting very tired at the time and wondered how long she could go on stalling, especially as she didn't know what Felipe had said.

But, whatever it was, it worked for both of them, because after Carla's evidence had been scrutinised, Felipe and she were released in the early hours. Evidently, Mercedes had been arrested.

Carla couldn't believe how many reporters were waiting for them outside the police station. The next thing Felipe did was phone the hospital to see how his mother was, but there was no change in her condition. That was another of the things that Carla loved about him. How he so obviously cared about his mother.

"I think we should go back to the yacht," he said. "I'll pull up the gangplank. They won't want to get their feet wet," he joked.

He had the yacht cleaned up and the late afternoon found them lying inside on the upper deck out of sight of the paparazzi, facing the sea. She turned over and studied him silently as he gazed into the azure sky from behind those dark inscrutable shades. She noticed with a pang that he still looked pale in spite of his tan and had several bruises showing on his cheek. She shivered momentarily, imagining what might have happened.

He must have been reading her thoughts because he turned to face her, took off his sunglasses and said, "You don't need to worry, Carla. Whoever was behind what happened over the last few days, will be thinking of making themselves scarce. The marina deal is definitely off. My visitors must have been in the pay of our past associates." His face was grim.

"What happened to them?" asked Carla. She'd been too preoccupied worrying about Felipe's position to think about the fate of those brutes.

"Evidently after leaving *La Paloma,* they got away. The police found black clothes and balaclavas dumped in the harbour. They'll get them though." His trust in the local force was comforting. She still couldn't get over how she'd managed to do what she had. Although it was only twenty-four hours, the trip to Mercedes's villa seemed like a dream now.

"And it's all thanks to you, Carla," he said, face lighting up.

"Thanks." She lay back and breathed in deeply, feeling relaxed at last. They didn't speak for a moment. She'd been very worried about the shop, but Felipe had suggested she asked Martina, the pharmacy assistant to look after it again. But she still had her future to think about. She turned her head and he was regarding her with a soft look in his eyes, while his finger traced the line of her arm, sending little electric shocks through her.

"If I keep asking Martina to look after the

shop, she won't want to give it up," she'd joked. "I should get back." His finger stopped stroking her and the rest of his hand was now holding her arm.

"You want to leave? Well?" he said. She smiled back at him uncertainly. Everything was moving so fast now, but she knew she had to keep her head. It was the first time since Jack died that she'd let any man into her life.

"You know you said the plans weren't going through . . . ?"

"Yes?"

"So my business is safe?" She was sorry after she said it, knowing it wasn't really the time to talk about this with his mother still lying unconscious in hospital.

"As far as I'm concerned."

"And what about your mother . . ." she hesitated. "I'm sorry. I'm being selfish."

"I understand perfectly. Don't worry, Carla. Things are going to work out for you."

"Are they?"

"If I have anything to do with it," he said. "And I intend to." She let him kiss her for a long time. She felt dizzy when he released her. She panicked a little then because of how she was feeling.

"I really should go, Felipe," she said,

brushing back her curls. He didn't reply, only gazed at her lovingly. All she wanted to do was throw herself back into his arms, but she couldn't. It wasn't the time.

Everything he said and did, pointed to how he was feeling, but she still wasn't sure, in spite of everything they had been through.

"Then you must," he said gently. "Anyway, I have to go and see Mother."

"I hope there's good news," she said. A moment later, he was on his feet and pulling her up. She slid easily into his arms.

"They'll soon call the newshounds off, with luck," he said, "but, for the present, I think we shall have to, as you say in English, run the gauntlet."

"That's very good, Felipe," said Carla, breaking the tension between them.

"Then, let's get going. I'll ring you from the hospital. And let Martina run the shop for another couple of days."

"I will." They went and gathered their things. Carla had slept in the stateroom when they got back. He had insisted on her having his bed. He had been the perfect gentleman.

She'd been quite exhausted after all the traumatic events, but she had woken several times, conscious of his closeness next door and wondered whether he thought her terribly old-fashioned for not agreeing to spend the night with him. But he had shown no sign of it.

As Carla packed her little bag, she wondered how long it would be until she would be back.

"Ready?" he asked. She nodded. "I've called for a car with a couple of my men to help us get away. We can't walk."

"I know." She wasn't used to being famous.

"There are more reporters and cameramen outside than I thought. I don't know how happy you're going to be about this, but I've been thinking. You can't possibly go back to your flat in the present climate. You'll be hounded. I suggest you stay with me at home." She opened her mouth to protest and he put a finger against her lips. "It's for the best. The villa is not a crime scene any longer. I've checked. And we do have the best security on the island. You'll be quite safe with me." Her heart lurched, but her senses were singing. She was going to be staying at the Villa Cristina with him.

"What about your mother?" she asked lamely.

"My mother would be in total agreement. And I'll go and see her this afternoon instead. That's settled then."

"What about my clothes?" He had that whimsical look on his face again.

"You'll find plenty of those at the villa. Anyway, you can always send for some more."

"Send?" she laughed incredulously.

"We'll worry about that after. Anyway, you look great. Now, are you ready," he repeated. "We might have to make a run for it. Give me your bag. My men are outside on the pontoon and the car's waiting."

A few seconds later, they were on the lower deck and Carla blinked at the crowd of pressmen and -women below. In all her wildest dreams, she had never expected to be the centre of such attention.

She saw Felipe nod and then they were down with the men closed around them. Soon, they were all sprinting towards a long, black car, with another parked behind it. Pursued by the press, they reached the open doors of the limo. "Phew," she said, collapsing inside, as Felipe jumped in behind her and the doors slammed shut.

"See what I mean," he said. She saw exactly what he meant. That he was important enough to be public property.

"They're not going to follow us, are they?" she asked, as she turned her head.

"Probably. But they'll have to camp outside the walls," he remarked, with a satisfied grin. "Are you all right?" He slipped his arm around her and she let her head fall into the hollow of his shoulder.

"Perfectly," she replied. And meant it.

A security man held open the car door for Carla and she stepped out into the wide space at the front of the Villa Cristina. How things change, she thought. The last time I was here none of this had happened!

A moment later, Felipe took her hand and squeezed it comfortingly. "Come on," he said. "You're safe here now."

Then the front door swung open to reveal Elise, Dona Alvarez's maid. Her face was pale and her expression anxious but, at the sight of Felipe, it collapsed into one huge grin. "It's so good to see you, sir." she cried. "I'm so glad that everything is all right. I knew you had nothing to do with it. My poor mistress!" She began to cry.

"Thank you, Elise," he replied, leading Carla towards her. "But you mustn't worry." He put a sympathetic arm around Elise's shoulders. "I know things look bad for Mother, but she's tough and I'm sure she's going to pull through. Please, no tears now, because I have a special task for you." Elise

134

sniffed. "Mrs Taylor is coming to stay for a few days."

Carla bore the maid's piercing look unflinchingly. "If it wasn't for her, I should be in prison now." Elise's brown eyes widened. "You've always looked after us all so well, now you must look after her." The maid nodded, shooting a nervous smile at Carla.

"I hope I won't be any trouble," said Carla in response. Felipe's eyebrows arched in amusement as he took her hand again and led her inside, followed by Elise. The security men had simply disappeared.

Once more, Carla was struck by the beauty of the place. Was she really going to stay here? It seemed impossible. She shook her head imperceptibly, but Felipe had noticed.

"You're tired, aren't you?"

"A little," she confessed. All of a sudden, what had happened was beginning to hit home.

"I want Mrs Taylor put in the Garden Room," he said.

"Yes, sir, I'll go and get it ready," replied Elise.

"And tell Cook, she's here, isn't she?, that we'd like some lunch on the terrace."

"I shall see it's your favourite," replied Elise. Her whole expression was completely different now, as if some great weight had been lifted from her. She hurried across the marble floor and disappeared.

"What is your favourite?" asked Carla. She wanted to know everything about him — what he ate, what he liked, about his family, absolutely everything. And it was only then that she realised she had fallen in love with him.

The notion was unbelievable as well as explosive. It was Jack she was in love with, but he wasn't coming back and the man standing before her had become inexplicably dear.

"What the matter?" Felipe asked.

"Nothing," she said, to cover her confusion. His brow wrinkled.

"You said you wanted to know what I like eating."

"Yes, I did." She smiled. "I suppose it's something exotic?" She was glad to concentrate on something trivial.

"No," he laughed. Then he wrinkled his nose deliciously. She just loved everything about him! "Well, partly."

"Go on then." She couldn't wait to hear.

"A good old-fashioned national dish. Paella followed by, more rare, black rice with sepia."

"Good heavens," she said. "How do you

make that?" They joked on, until Elise came back and led Carla away to the Garden Room.

She stepped inside, but as soon as she was on her own she threw herself down on the bed. "Wow, wow, wow!" she said out loud and lay back against the nest of feather-filled pillows.

The Garden Room looked out on to the pool. A few steps and you could be swimming lazily in the blue water. The room was fashioned of cool green marble, faintly Roman with slim pilasters holding up the ceiling; it was also Spanish Moorish with two deep recesses under ornamented arches. She got up and looked inside one of them. They turned out to be spacious walk-in wardrobes. One held men's clothes! Then she visited the other.

Felipe had been right. There were plenty of fantastic dresses and colourful separates, from evening to casual, and all designer. Probably for guests, who've lost their suitcases on the plane, she thought wryly, shaking her head.

"Phew!" She'd walked into the en suite, which was a huge green wet room sporting a corner bath and jacuzzi, a shower and every gadget going. All the taps and accessories were gold. It was heaven. Suddenly, she felt very scruffy and quite dowdy.

Half an hour later, she'd gone mad and tried on some of the outfits, but now she was finally wrapped in the most luxurious robe she'd ever worn. Then she lay down on the bed, staring out at the azure pool, deciding whether she dared to swim. But that would mean another trip to the wet room — and maybe a jacuzzi. She couldn't make her mind up which!

She was so deep in frivolous thought that she jumped as she heard a tap on the door. "It's only me," said Felipe. She hurried over. Her heart thumping. She should have dressed instead of lounging about in someone else's home.

"May I come in?" He looked down at her. He was smiling, as his dark eyes strafed her body. "Do you like all this?" he gestured, grinning.

"Oh, yes," she replied enthusiastically.

"I'm glad," he said, taking her in his arms. He was wearing the most wonderful aftershave, that made her senses swirl. "You deserve spoiling."

"Thank you," she said, savouring his nearness. "Actually, it's absolute heaven!" She smiled back into his eyes.

"I'm not keen on it myself," he said. "I like my hammock." There came an abrupt halt by a sharp knocking.

"Sir, it's Elise."

"What is it," he asked, rushing over and opening the door a tiny crack.

"It's the hospital! On the phone." Elise handed it through.

Carla froze. Please don't let anything have happened to his mother, she prayed. He stood attentively, listening. A moment later, his expression was pure excitement.

"It's all right. Mother's regained consciousness and she's asking for me. I really should have been there. Do you mind, darling? Elise will look after you."

"Of course not. You go!"

"I'll ring you." A moment later, he was bounding through the door.

Carla lay back on the sumptuous bed, her heart thudding. Once again, nothing had happened between them, but she was still singing inside. He'd called her darling!

Then her spirits fell abruptly and guilt set in. Yes, he should have been with his mother! And what would Dona Ximene think about her being in the villa alone with him? Doubts came crowding in. How suitable a girlfriend could she be for the Dona's precious only son?

An hour later, Carla was sitting on the terrace, picking at the most fabulous paella she'd ever tasted and taking tiny forkfuls of the piquant black rice that he said he loved so much. How much did she wish that he was with her! Then her mobile rang.

"Felipe? How's your mother?" Carla was so relieved when she heard the news . . .

"She wants to meet you," he said.

"Are you sure?" asked Carla doubtfully.

"Yes, and to thank you for all you've done for us."

"There's no need," said Carla. "Anyone with an ounce of sense would have thought about taking a duplicate."

"I don't think so," he replied. "I didn't. Anyway, Mother wants to see you."

"When?"

"A couple of days. I could have told you when I got back, but I wanted to now!"

After two wonderful days, they went to see Dona Ximene. Carla had done as Felipe suggested, and sent for some clothes! She didn't really want to turn up at the hospital wearing something from his mother's guest wardrobe!

She chose a conservative dress; a fashionable print, sprigged with flowers and a beige linen jacket from the ten outfits that were delivered to her door by the owner of a very smart boutique positioned near the Town

Hall. Then the owner advised a pretty pair of high-heeled sandals and matching bag.

When she was alone, Carla hardly knew herself.

"You look wonderful," Felipe said.

"You don't look too bad yourself," she smiled. He was wearing a beige linen suit that complemented her jacket. "Did you know what I was going to buy? We look like twins!"

"I'm glad we're not," he responded with a cheeky grin. Carla still couldn't help blushing at the intensity of his gaze. "And Mother is going to love you. Like I do." She closed her eyes as he held her tightly and kissed her. "Sorry, I don't want to crease you." He apologised.

"I don't mind," she replied and blushed again. Which was quite ridiculous, seeing she'd been married.

"Let's go then," he said, extending his hand. She took it and they walked out of the room together and through the front door where the Porsche was waiting. He'd got the car back from the police.

The hospital was as lovely a place as any hospital could be — white and bright with flowers in the foyer and nurses all dressed in white with blue piping, gliding about the place.

"It's lovely," she said involuntarily, remembering how much she'd hated hospitals, which always reminded her of Jack.

"I don't know about that," he said. "Mother has a private room, of course. And she's making her presence known," Felipe went on. "She likes her own way, I'm afraid. And doesn't suffer fools gladly."

But as they walked towards the Dona's room, Carla's stomach was turning over and over. He must have sensed her nervousness as he gripped her hand firmly, giving her courage. But she was still anxious that Dona Ximene would not approve of her son and an ordinary English girl getting together.

The Dona was seated propped against a pile of pillows — not in bed, but an easy chair. Felipe handed her the flowers he had brought for her, not from the florist's, but consisting of a simple bouquet that Carla had picked from her own garden. "Thank you, dear," she said to him, burying her face in to take the scent. "Now . . ." she extended both her hands. "Now, Mrs Taylor, come here."

"Carla, please." She went forward. To her amazement, the lady drew her down and kissed her on both cheeks. Her perfume was both delicate and expensive. "Sit down here, please, Carla." She indicated a nearby chair.

Carla settled herself as comfortably as she could, given the situation, while Felipe sat down on the other side of his mother. "I want to thank you from the depths of my soul," she continued. "You saved Xavier and I am so very grateful." She smiled, then drew her brows together. "To think he could have been accused! My son! I want him to prosecute our stupid police for false arrest."

"I don't think so, Mother," said Felipe. "I'd rather lie low." He glanced at Carla as if to say, see what I mean. She's fully recovered! Carla didn't know how to respond, only smiled and nodded idiotically!

"Xavier tells me you have been staying at the villa to keep him company?"

"Yes, I have and it's been wonderful."

"I'm glad," replied his mother surprisingly. "Xavier needs intelligent female company." Carla blinked, wondering what was coming next. "He has always . . ." the Dona grimaced, ".. always . . . and he will not be happy when I say this . . . picked the wrong kind of girlfriend."

"Has he?" asked Carla, trying not to smile at how uncomfortable Felipe looked.

"Take that Mercedes! Oh, that woman! I shall write to her mother."

"I don't think you should do that," said Felipe.

"Are you advising me as my lawyer, or my son?"

"I think — your son," said Felipe, making a face. "Anyway, Carla doesn't want to hear any more about it, do you, Carla?"

"Mm, I don't know," replied Carla mischievously. A moment later, Dona Ximene threw her head back and laughed.

"I see you understand, Carla. We shall get along fine." Carla felt hugely relieved. "I thought that when I first met you. You have a good business head on your shoulders. And — now to business."

"Should you tire yourself, Mother?" asked Felipe looking anxious.

"Nonsense!" said Dona Ximene. "I can't wait to get out of here. And Carla wants to know what's going to happen to her shop?"

"Very much!" she said enthusiastically. "But only if you're up to it."

"The project is off," the old lady continued. Felipe held Carla's eyes with his I told you so. "But I do have some plans for the front. How would you like to run a bigger business, dear?"

"Pardon?"

"I've always quite fancied another up-market boutique like the one in the square." Dona Ximene was looking over Carla's outfit. She'd evidently recognised the brand.

144

"But bigger, much bigger."

"Mother!" remonstrated Felipe. "You have to get well first."

"But Carla is entirely well. She and I shall go into business. You may say what you like but, as I said, I have plans for your Mrs Taylor. And you cannot stand between a woman and her plans."

"Don't I know it," said Felipe.

"It will do you good, my son." He lifted a quizzical eyebrow. "To have a girlfriend in business. It will make a change from lawyers." He grinned in spite of himself. "Now, Carla, what do you think of my plan?"

"I can't believe it," she replied, thinking how nervous she'd been when she entered. "But I'm very interested."

"That's settled then," said Dona X. "Now I am feeling tired. Take Carla away, Felipe, and be nice to her."

"Oh, I intend to," he said.

9

The fairy lights looked even more beautiful tossing in the tangled branches of the trees, than they had the first time he had taken her to his favourite restaurant. She smiled at him. "It seems ages since we came here. And all the things that have happened!" She could hardly believe it.

"It isn't that long," he said, bringing the car to a halt. He smiled at her and patted her arm gently.

"Why are we here?" she asked, although she knew the answer to her question already. That first date had been magical and they both wanted the magic to last. And she had fallen in love with him, although she didn't really know it then. She remembered her thoughts at the time. I could fall in love with him, if I wasn't still in love with Jack. What had changed? Maybe it was because Felipe was in love with her too?

"We need to eat?" he replied, but his eyes

told her something else. Soon, his warm arm was guiding her through the pretty porch and a moment later, they were met inside by the owner, who looked smarter than ever, but much less intimidating than the last time Carla had stood beside Felipe. She was so much more confident now.

"I am so happy to see you, Senor Alvarez," he said, offering his hand.

"Thank you, Pedro," Felipe said, shaking it warmly.

"And, of course, I welcome your beautiful companion." Carla smiled at his obvious sincerity.

"Thank you," she said. She could see how much Felipe was admired — and not only for his custom.

"Maria!" called Pedro. A pretty girl appeared and, with a tiny curtsy, offered Carla an exquisite small bouquet.

"How lovely!" She sniffed the blooms appreciatively, savouring their fragrance.

"They are all island flowers," remarked Felipe. "Unfortunately, Pedro, I have no reservation."

"Your usual table is waiting, senor," Pedro smiled. "It has been kept free since . . ." he shrugged ". . . since you were unable to visit us . . . but I always knew you would be returning." He led them into the restaurant, which was almost full, and indicated the same spot on the terrace, where they had sat and gazed across at the view.

A moment later, to Carla's astonishment and Felipe's evident embarrassment, spontaneous applause rippled around the restaurant. Then a couple got up and came over. Carla recognised the elegant woman immediately.

"Dona Ana." Felipe greeted her with a kiss on both cheeks. A moment later, Carla was welcomed in a similar fashion by her companion, a tall distinguished grey-haired man with a moustache.

"Antonio and I want to say that we never believed any of that rubbish about you, Xavier," enthused Dona Ana. "I can't tell you how relieved we are to know dear Ximene is recovering. We all feel this." She looked around. "You are among friends."

Felipe smiled, then held up his hand. "I know that." He turned to face the diners. "Thank you, my friends. I am as glad to be here, as you are to see me. But I would like you to know that if it had not been for Carla," he turned back and looked at her with shining eyes, "things might have been very different."

"Then we have much to thank you for, Carla," said Senor Antonio, "this young man is very precious to us all."

"I think so," Carla said, looking up at Felipe. It was the first time she had seen him truly embarrassed.

"You are much loved, senor," added Pedro. Carla found herself thinking what restaurateur in England or what diners would have behaved in such an emotional way. "I hope too the Dona is recovering well."

"She is, Pedro. Thank you." Felipe nodded, a relieved smile on his face. A moment later, they embraced Dona Ana and her husband again and walked across to the table. Carla could feel every eye upon her, but she didn't care now about anything. Except that she was with him.

"It's so high up here," she said involuntarily, as she sat down. It had been her first thought when last she had taken her seat on the terrace. His eyes twinkled as if he remembered.

The sun had already set and, below, the valley was a great black void, punctuated by dots of light that competed with the myriads of stars above. It was like taking a seat in space. The air was warm and the breeze's light fingers only ruffled their hair.

"Thank you," he said, leaning forward. She looked at him in surprise.

"What for?"

"For making everything right."

"How have I done that?" asked Carla shakily.

"You know how," he said.

"I only duplicated the evidence." She made an attempt to joke.

"I don't mean that," he replied. "I mean . . ." he stopped.

"Yes?" She found her heart was pounding.

"I mean that ever since I met you, my life has been different."

"How?" She wanted him to say it; to hear what she wanted to hear above everything.

"Because I am a man in love. For the first time in my whole life!" He said it firmly and sincerely. A few short weeks ago, she would never have believed it. But she knew it was true.

"I am too," she said quietly. "Only . . . once . . ."

"Yes?"

". . . Once I thought I could never love again, but now I know that isn't true. Although it's all like a dream."

"What is?" he asked softly.

"All this," she indicated, "the view, the place. . . . You? But I haven't forgotten Jack . . ."

"I know," he said. "He can't be replaced. I don't want to take his special place in your heart, but I would like a little space."

"You have it," she said. He reached out and took her hand and placed it against his shirt, so she could feel his heart beating. He was so romantic!

The dinner went well and neither she nor Felipe had eyes for anyone, but each other. After the exquisite food, which included black rice with sepia, they leaned back to relax with their coffees. Both stared out across the landscape.

"You know how I think of this place . . ." began Carla, ". . . no, not the restaurant — the island. We . . . Jack and I . . . called it, *Our Island of Dreams* and that's why I came, to realise that dream. And now I've found it. Of course, he's not here anymore, but I know he'd be happy for me."

Felipe was silent for a moment, then he said, "It has always been my island of dreams as well, Carla. Wherever I have travelled in the world, I wanted to come back home, but, now, it is even more perfect." He was fidgeting, which wasn't like him.

A moment later, he produced something from his pocket. Carla's eyes opened wide. "And it would be even more perfect, if you would accept this." He handed over the tiny red box. She stared at it. "You know I love you. Please open it."

It was the most glorious diamond she had ever seen. She gasped.

"Do you like it?" he asked anxiously.

"Yes, it's fantastic but . . ."

"Carla, will you marry me?" He was beside her and ready to drop on his knee. She was almost dazed; and then everything became extremely clear, as if she'd never seen anything so clearly before.

"Yes, yes, of course I will. Please get up, Felipe." He kissed her hand, then stood up, bent over and kissed her on the lips.

They were oblivious to the hush that had fallen over the restaurant. But then wild clapping brought them back to earth. Carla's cheeks were scarlet as Felipe went back to his seat and smiled at her. "I'm sorry for that very public proposal," he said, "but I can do it again, if you like. In private."

"Yes, please," she said, smiling back. A few minutes later, as Carla began to regain her composure, she added, "Felipe, there are two things I want to know."

"Of course," he replied looking surprised.

"First, should I call you Xavier?" He burst out laughing.

"Call me anything you like, my darling,"

he said. "And?" He lifted his eyebrows quizzically.

"Ever since you came into my shop, the first time I saw you, I've been wondering who you bought that pashmina for." He laughed out loud.

"You silly girl. It's still wrapped in its pretty paper in the boot of my car. It was the only excuse I could find to get to talk to you. Would you like another coffee?"

"Yes, please," she said. While he was ordering, she looked out across the valley and breathed a slight prayer: *Wherever you are, Jack, I know you want me to be happy. And I am. Truly I am.*

We hope you have enjoyed this Large Print book. Other Thorndike, Wheeler, Kennebec, and Chivers Press Large Print books are available at your library or directly from the publishers.

For information about current and upcoming titles, please call or write, without obligation, to:

Publisher
Thorndike Press
295 Kennedy Memorial Drive
Waterville, ME 04901
Tel. (800) 223-1244

or visit our Web site at:

http://gale.cengage.com/thorndike

OR

Chivers Large Print
published by BBC Audiobooks Ltd
St James House, The Square
Lower Bristol Road
Bath BA2 3SB
England
Tel. +44(0) 800 136919
email: bbcaudiobooks@bbc.co.uk
www.bbcaudiobooks.co.uk

All our Large Print titles are designed for easy reading, and all our books are made to last.